Leonore Griebel

Leonore Griebel

Hermann Stehr

K A Nitz
LOWER HUTT

Leonore Griebel first published
in German 1900

This translation by Kerry Nitz
Copyright © K A Nitz 2012
All rights reserved

ISBN: 978-0-473-22014-3

National Library of New Zealand Cataloguing-
in-Publication Data

Stehr, Hermann, 1864-1940.
Leonore Griebel / by Hermann Stehr ;
translated by Kerry Nitz.
ISBN 978-0-473-22014-3
I. Title.
833.91—dc 23

*To the poet
Gerhart Hauptmann,
dedicated in deep
reverence.*

But we are fated
To rest in no place,
Suffering men
Fading away, falling
At random from one
Hour to the next,
Like water tossed
From crag to crag
For years into the unknown.
        Hölderlin: Hyperion's Song of Fate

CHAPTER 1

Leonore Griebel

There are strong families whose lives play out in the same shape through centuries. Their ancestors' principles oblige and constrain wordlessly just like the blind laws of matter build up the soundness of the body.

The cloth maker Joseph Griebel of Altenrode was descended from such a family.

The large house on Walkergasse in which he lived had been there as long as anyone could remember. The same people were always going in and out through the double front doors. Portly men, with peculiarly short, fat legs, slow and dignified — and their large hands caressing their fat cheeks from time to time as their blue eyes gazed mildly and tenderly.

The mothers and daughters were tall and wide hipped, suited to activity, with tough, direct faces over which a stern trait laid itself over time.

But it was strange. The house experienced the family's history vicariously. Not so that it entirely merged into it, no, in mysterious ways it lowered the force of its established existence into the plastic souls of the people who came lastingly into the forbidding circle of its foundations.

Every time an old man had gone to the graveyard, the young wife filled its wide, high-ceilinged rooms with laughter. She adorned the high windows with white curtains and wrung a jovial tone out of the stiff, cold walls with her zest for life.

Then the great doors would move swinging gently. The front doors would break open and the light would drive away the cold humidity with its sunny breath. In the same way, the treads of the stairs themselves creaked teasingly when fleet little children's feet hurried over them, and the curves of the bronzed banister purred with pleasure as a result. Even the old lion's head at the end of the stairs, which roared at the street so grimly with throat wide open, would blink archly with rigid eyes in whose corners was laid the crust of its great age.

Yes, the old building was even becoming gossipy. It enticed the children into the darkness of its contorted garrets. They were filled with many dusty chests and drawers in which faded garments lay: mobcaps with flowery ribbons and dull gold trim, corsets, hooped skirts, long, blue, severe cloth coats with dignified, wide lapels.

Then it would tell the children faded stories, sweet, ornate fairytales. It would take groaning breathes with its wide chimneys so as to then mutter away again in the humming, warm silence. But the little ones would sit before the colourful things and listen with bright eyes.

The old life danced across the floor of the garrets in high heels with fluttering skirts and flying ribbons. It strode in in breeches and beat the rattan cane slowly. Only when it met a limb, it would sound shrilly and the entire presence suddenly disappear.

In the rooms below, which were not so cold and dismal anymore now either, the young wife of easy gait walked about and the young master smiled a quiet, peaceful smile.

The sun raised its bright joy over the ancient, large house and painted its glistening rings on its cold grey with happily trembling golden fingers so that the house quaked in restrained bliss, and it encouraged the trees of the spacious garden from their deep absorption. The old pear tree, under which the arbour stood, was laughing once more with its pitiful branches and adorning itself with a sparse posy of white blossoms. The young saplings though were swaying in the dance of a soft breeze and throwing the exuberance of their red-blossoming youth in handfuls onto the grass.

The people of Altenrode were shaking their heads because they could not grasp the change which had taken place before their eyes with the old house on Walkergasse.

Not a soul, even including the occupants, knew that it had its relapses into its innate, stiff, weighty seriousness.

It was never completely cast off, not even with the sweetest smile of the youngest child. For in the most hidden depths of its inner being, it lay undamped in its cellars. It dwelt there captive, but suddenly, often on the most joyous days, when the heel of a striding foot stamped too hard on the marble of the hall, it flared up and lumbered turbidly up the stairs into all the rooms. Then a secret grumble awoke in such corners where it had hidden away resting, and it stretched into low hard sounds.

And when the little lamp in the child's room, that vigilant mother's eye, was then extinguished because it had no cradle anymore to repulse the terror from, the house's grim soul recovered its old might more and more.

It ventured with monotonous, hard contours into every night as it had always done formerly, and even the moon was not in a position to wipe the air of proud acerbity from its grey brow. And every hard, rough thought awoke in its rooms. With the tall, deep shadows of its high-ceilinged rooms, it stooped over the beds of the sleeping and whispered murky dreams into their souls. The adults only stirred sighing in their beds; the children started frightened and stared fearfully into the night. But they heard nothing but the solitary clock in the hall ticking away and they fell asleep without fear again.

In the morning everyone was depressed and said that they had a bad night.

That's why they became accustomed to a soft, gliding gait and communicated in whispers, often only by hand gestures or the countenance of their eyes. The homecoming children did well to scare up the house from its lonely chill so that it answered their young voices with cheerful, soulful sounds.

But these cheerful hours became less and less frequent.

The laughing spirits were leaving the house by and by. In the end, in all the souls and rooms, an earthy sobriety reigned, an earnest dutifulness, a strict usefulness and a hard conventionality, the unsophisticated spirit of that long forgotten progenitor who had erected the house.

The white curtains disappeared from the windows which now looked indifferently into the distance again with their black glass. The rooms became unadorned and drab. The stairs lay there taciturnly. The lion's head at their end lost all good-natured expression. Only occasionally did the double doors open. In the lower hall, the old, damp stuffiness lay again.

Self-confident, in snobbish pride, the large house towered over the tiny little houses to the left and right. And while they were arduously blowing thin threads of smoke from narrow chimneys, their large neighbour was puffing mighty clouds. The breaths of its draughts were travelling heavily through its massive chimney.

The tradition of his house had been disturbed by old Konstantin Griebel. He had only acquiesced to die after turning eighty and it had not happened in the accustomed manner either. Instead of extinguishing quietly with a blissful face as a blessing, a wild unrest had come over him as death tore him away from the unfinished repast of life.

His son had stood by the bed shocked and had forgotten to close the dead man's eyes which were staring goggle-eyed at him as though in a stifled scream of reproach. But then he cautiously stroked the eyelids over the empty, anxious eyes and went out trembling.

"He wanted to say something to me," he pondered. "But what was it? Didn't sound like ha..., like: Son, make ... only? What did it mean then, that he was looking at me with his eyes in deathly fear when he'd already died?"

And he could not expunge from his ears the agonising slurring of the dying man, and was constantly seeing the horror of the broken eyes.

And when the deceased had been carried out by his guild companions, when all smell of the funeral had died away in the broad calm of the large house, it did not change.

One day something quite strange took place. He was stepping down the stairs, thinking about his work, his blue apron tied around him, and suddenly felt the blind urge within himself to look up. But, what was that in the hall?! — — It could not be from the two round windows in the front doors: two tired eyes were lying on the well-worn floor tiles. Across their half-extinguished blue trembled a dull glassy gleam, glistening rings were climbing from their depths and dispersing softly on the surface like faltering tears.

So that his shirt barely rustled, the cloth maker turned around, waved the almost deaf housekeeper from the kitchen and pointed out the apparition to her with shaking arm.

But she did not understand, shook her head and at the same time wiped her thin nose with two fingers.

"There!" he breathed.

"What?" she finally cried with bodily strength in the way the deaf do.

By the coarse sound, however, the decaying blue began to gently slip away, and when he again pointed at it more urgently, "There!", it had already become the two splotches of light which always lay in the damp hall.

"There," she cried, "those, hm, those are lights from the two windows. Nothing more. Nothing else at all. Yes. — And you, Mr Josef, I want to tell you, it'll be best for you if you marry."

"Window lights?" he said inwardly to himself. "Me? Marry? ... Haha! — And when the women become as old as sawdust, they know no different. — Me? — Well yes, yes, some day. — But now, soon, at once? No! When I have turned thirty-eight, I can also turn thirty-nine. No, no. — But it may be! Something just isn't right anymore since father died."

With that the old housekeeper turned around, and while she slowly shuffled out, she laughed weakly and waggled her head.

But he walked to the front door and carefully dodged the patches as he did so. However, each of the patches had nevertheless been a short while ago a tired, weeping eye.

And he defied the demand stipulated by his family's tradition, whose unrefusability he set against only the ease of his increasing age so long as it worked. His father had also perhaps wanted the same from him during the torment of his last restive days.

At last these thoughts also came to the old housekeeper, and she immediately admonished the procrastinator,

"Look, you don't have to do anything differently. I knew your blessed father when he was a young hare. Yes, and like his father, I mean your grandfather, it was fourteen days before All Saints' Day, and he lay dying, and his breath went in gasps, no, then your blessed father came to the bed with his sweetheart who became your mother. You should have seen how he smiled contentedly! He gave them his hand and said, 'Now I want to die, children,' he said, smiled once more and died.

You see, Mr Josef, that's just it! Why couldn't he die? — Hey? Because a man without a wife just isn't right. It just doesn't come to anything! And in time it matts up in such a man and he pokes in it like a finger pokes in a mouth and he bites his hand off with his teeth without realising."

"Ha! And it simply bites you sometimes too, as much as one can hear. Hahaha!" Josef replied, laughing maliciously.

"Now, Josef, stop horsing around! It's not funny. Truly isn't, my soul. The house is dying without a lady. Take note, sir!"

In fact, it appeared as though the old house was fed up once again with its deep loneliness and was longing for a human springtime to be skipping on little children's feet through its rooms. So sore voices became loud, so it talked crooning with its tall doors, so it intimidated with its long shadows, so it called wistfully with the deathly silence of its large rooms. Finally the cloth maker did not enjoy its desolation anymore either. The yearning after his youth was awakening in him. In this hankering, he married.

The old housekeeper who had argued for it so bravely, did not live to see it. She died shortly before the wedding.

CHAPTER 2

Leonore Griebel

His young wife was Leonore, maiden name Marsel.

Her long-deceased father had been the last offshoot of a baronial house that had been impoverished for generations, Karl August Theodor von Marsel, baker by trade.

He had sold his bread without fuss and with a shy, sheepish face from one of the small houses on Walkergasse.

A series of his forefathers had become wild and grand through the lustre of the distant past. The narrow spaces of hardship had gradually broken the proud wings of the bearers of the great name, and the yearning lay in them like an unavoidable sorrow, a pointless, continually renewed torment.

They atrophied bit by bit next to the small windows and the paltry household utensils. The scanty dinner sucked the strength from them, and the soundness and fullness of their bodies dwindled under the merciless pressure of plain garments.

The harmony of their powerful limbs degenerated into morbid daintiness. The long, free gait narrowed into shuffling, and the play of pretty hands staled into snobbish grimaces.

— With their soul's wounds, they sired their children and they served them the poison of their vanity as the milk of the first legends.

The most secret, deepest life of their heart became a powerlessly trembling, weak tone.

Only their beautiful hair was passed over by the decline of their family. Yes, the more inconsolable its wreckage became, the richer flowed the fullness of its sheen.

And even their large, softly singing eyes were adorning the hidden delusion in which they were wasting away.

In the last of the diminished stock, the baker Karl August Theodor, the wounds had become empty of blood; the vanity had become a dry, choking fever.

This was just enough for the soul of a delicate girl whose life was at risk of being extinguished like a flame.

The father received the news of her birth when already lying on his deathbed. A fright made him even paler. Then he motioned with his hand to the midwife to come closer,

"Leonore Marie von Marsel," his lips breathed and a weak smile curved his mouth.

Leonore Griebel

With the sympathy of small souls, which so humbles, the residents of Walkergasse made it possible for the young widow to continue the business of her husband with the help of a former assistant.

Broken in the prime of her hope, amounting to the fulfillment of her desire by fate, always fighting for her child's life with the concealed weapons of maternal sorrow, she became a limb of the unfortunate family which in her man had fled with weak convulsions under the earth.

He had died in the period of the marriage where the understanding is still powerless against the images that young blood inscribes in the heart. So his image and the history of his family assumed exaggerated dimensions and colours in her imagination.

The piecemeal stories from his memory sounded again in her like mysterious great tones which carried a whiff of genteel distance. The ugly noises of the fall of debris remained hidden from her.

Her soul kept vigil over Leonore, her only child, like ailing dawn over a wilting flower.

Only on Sundays, when the holiday light was playing in idle beauty before the quiet, little bakery, did she spin fairy tales in the avidly dreaming soul of the little girl. During the week, when industriousness rushed in clattering clogs through the narrow rooms, the child would then memorise the stories she had heard in thousands of secret plays.

Leonore was too frail to take part in rough games with neighbouring children of a similar age. The instinct for her frailty also held her back from it. Her mother had to feed the hunger of her imagination always with the ancient, great stories which she had retained from her husband's tellings.

Thus the narrow life of early childhood was lost to Leonore, as was the wholesomeness of direct fluctuations, the freshness of self-actioned experience.

Her inner being became comprised of self-indulgent, twilight spaces, mysterious vibrations, secret, unworldly sounds and colours, a store of infinitely hazy schemes to which nothing was attached, which could produce nothing clearly active.

Sitting silently, playing with her long, thin fingers in her lap whilst gazing into the expanse which lay behind all matter, she was happy.

When her mother noticed what her love had wreaked, it was already too late to fix.

The girl was now only kept to any domestic tasks by force. She also gave in to the commands of her mother, swept, laundered, stood behind the counter, helped with baking. But she did it with the suffering, secret reluctance of a weak nature.

Leonore Griebel

She bore this animated life with its loud, inconsiderate commands; restive, swarming wishes; burning questions; and heavy decisions like an irksome rattle. And the further it penetrated into her through practice and fixed itself with rigour, the more ardent was the springing back into the many-coloured, delicate, incorporeal mystery of her innermost soul.

She would have liked to have talked in long bell peals. It was a deep-reaching relaxation in her, like wafting wind, washing waves.

If a mysterious roaring awoke in the heavens which noiselessly pleated the clouds like large, stiff garments and extorted from the trees an earnest, low bowing, then she felt healthy and at home.

Derision had robbed her of pride in the noble name to her mother's joy. The tales of her childhood disappeared under the noise of more arduous, often more squalid years. It never crossed her mind later to want to be anyone but the daughter of the baker Marsel.

But with hidden tears, with anxiety and the constricting feeling of strangeness and desolation, she bore the split in her nature.

Her body was just as discordant, and delicate. But it was not the rounded daintiness of a bird. For as soon as she took a step, the play of her long arms spread a stiff dignity over the pointed mobility of limbs which touched on the comical.

Hermann Stehr

A dry magic lay in her body which was missing all feminine fullness. Her full hair had the colour of the tired November sun.

One of her soft-blue, singing eyes lay half-obscured by a weak eyelid and often stood rigidly while the other moved gently as though by its movements a mysterious song was ringing out from the self-indulgent, twilight spaces of her soul.

CHAPTER 3

Leonore Griebel

Joseph Griebel was without any alienation. His modest hopes had continually found ready circumstances. Never in his life had he come to deep, feverish breaths. He had relished his years like an always consistently baked bread.

His father's laws were the laws of his will.

He differed from him like a younger from an older timber. He lay in his place trimmed, trued up, dried out, solid, with all the conventional edges and flourishes provided, only in lighter, more sensitive colours.

His father's death had carried him to it with hurried, foundering grasp and a few shaking blows of his gavel.

Then a groaning and gnashing had passed through the tough frame of his being, and a long, deep tone was awoken in the wood of his soul by the hammer blows of death. He was reproducing himself through every cell of his past, and when he had finally reached the thin pithy threads of his youth, a last breath of yearning came out with an ever quieter, though narrower quivering. The thin thread of animated type began once more to vibrate in sympathy with the warmer pulse of already tired juices.

Muted images smouldered to him through a white, delicate veil with faded, chaste colours. A flood of gentle tones lay in the scent that emanated from him.

Since his being had not become mistrustful by a misstep, doubting through a disappointment, knotted by an emotional entanglement, he rose in his clumsily brimming wholesomeness and recklessly abandoned himself to gentle, beautiful rapture. Under the influence of this last, warming glance of the spring sun, the earnest, ready timber assumed once more the form of a man.

His entire conventional, serviceable, sober life seemed like a great void to him. Only the delicate, the unfamiliar, the quiet had any weight for him. Thus he had to find Leonore.

Like a spring flower which has coaxed a propitious November out of the feeble earth, he found her.

And he carried her home with shaking hand into the great, lifeless void of his life. The serious house on Walkergasse took her in with the most joyful booming of its many-chambered, broad breast.

CHAPTER 4

Leonore Griebel

Leonore always encountered life quite help-lessly. She would be beating the wings of her desire, but fate would then came and lead her somewhere else entirely, like a bird buffeted by a storm. Her heart would then beat in anxious curiosity whilst the wind of fate filled the sails of her existence.

"Marry, mother?" she asked and shook her head slowly, as she understood nothing.

A mild evening lay in the bakery, and the yellow shelves which reached to the ceiling were smouldering dully through the clear darkness.

Her mother was sitting behind the counter The girl was leaning on it propped on her elbows.

"Marry ..." she repeated quite timidly.

"Well yes, you are twenty."

"But why?"

With that she stood and walked through the narrow room from the door to the flour bags on the opposite wall a couple of times.

But her mother laughed reflectively and fell silent for a while.

"Aren't you fine with him?" she then asked.

Leonore paused and looked at the ground pondering.

"Fine? ... fine? ..." and she slowly hunched her skinny shoulders, "Yes!" she said, doubting, unknowing.

The evening bells awoke gently with the high singing of the little bells and then stretched to slow, solemn breaths with the full clanging of the heavier bells.

They both listened with hands clasped. Finally the sound disappeared with a soft trembling in the air.

"I would think the man must also have bells inside himself," Leonore began again.

"Why should that be?"

"Oh, I don't really know why myself, but to me it's really just like a town in which no bells don't toll. And why does he take me just now."

"Life is just like that. — Silly thing, didn't your father marry me too?"

"Yes, you and father!"

"Well, how is it with you then, girl?"

"When?"

"When he comes."

"Then he simply comes."

"And when he goes?"

"The same."

"Nothing more? — Nothing? — Not even joy that he goes?"

"Why should I rejoice then? No ... no ... That would be stupid. But because of what I said just now, it would have to really toll with bells in us, don't you think, mother?"

"Well, come, girl. I would think it's already tolling in you ..." The shop bell stirred. A customer entered and her mother had to break off the conversation.

Leonore went out through the other door.

But her mother was not mistaken. Those mysterious vibrations were awakening in the girl once more and they came wandering from far within her and brought with them the hankering for the scents from which a robust life must forbear. But all that had nothing to do with the relationship to Griebel, not even with her life. They originated from the reflection of her own hidden thought connections and then went disruptively through the visible existence which she was living puppet-like without any undertone.

If she rose then everything which she was familiar with and had experienced shrunk in her. And straits and strife preoccupied her. It seemed to her as though she was hanging in the air. She walked as though on sinking ground, scared, timid, without aim.

In such moods, she liked to go into the church. It brought her peace again.

The high, dusky vaults; the colourful, solemn-
ly untroubled light; that entirely unworldly,
unfamiliar scent which flowed from everything;
that lack of restraint which everything tended
towards — it all returned her belief in herself, the
feeling of a great power.

Then her life was no longer aching. For her
inner being had won an external foothold. Not by
a clear formulation of her catholic confession,
but rather by the emptying of a broad, silent
stream from an inner constriction uninhibited
into an external one.

Between these two glimmering expanses, she
walked the incomprehensible path of her life
with anxious curiosity and awe.

Standing like houses by its sides were classes,
virtues, vices, age, dreams, hopes, love, honour,
learning. People went in and out of these houses,
talked a language whose deepest meaning she
did not understand, laughed and got annoyed,
were happy and wasted away.

She was not exactly familiar with anything but
the love of her mother. Then a loud tone from
solid ground climbed out of her and flooded back
into her. It was the only power in her, although
she also only comprehended a small part of her
undiscovered being. But all the veiled effective
powers of her soul bowed to this imperative.

And since her mother desired it, Leonore let
herself be borne by Joseph Griebel's shaking

hand into the house of matrimony. At the same time, a tremor was convulsing her body and her heart.

The shaking of the man's hand was increased by it.

Leonore sensed then that a power over her husband resided in her.

She enjoyed this feeling gliding over her like an unaccountable lust.

CHAPTER 5

Leonore Griebel

The large house had rejoiced on the wedding day with the violins of the musicians, with the laughter of the young girls, with the deep broad sounds from the joyous chests of men.

Then deep in the night, without discernible cause, an unfriendly weariness had come over the building.

The sober guests felt it, rose hastily from their places and wished the bride and groom a good night, whereat the men laughed loudly and as a result were struck on the back by the women. The young girls, however, stole away with red cheeks.

Around two o'clock the last drunks, knotted into a large troop partly for safety, staggered out the front door onto the street and immediately began singing:

Red sky, red sky,
Light my way to die.

The house groaned vexedly for a while with the rusted hinges of its doors, then at daybreak it breathed its most wondrous dreams over the souls of the young couple.

The Marsel baker had wanted by all means to give her daughter a trousseau. But it had remained undone at Griebel's request.

"Oh mother, where would I put the things then! Everywhere has more than enough of everything. Better that you keep it. Then if something is left over in the end, it isn't lost to us."

So Leonore had nothing to make the settling in easy for her. No soft song was toned by familiar utensils from her past and could thus bind her new life to her old. It seemed to her as though she had leapt over a chasm. She was quite timid and uncertain amidst the wealth and affluence whose mistress she now had to be. — In addition, she had never lived her early life with the seriousness and attentiveness which comes from within. All the years of her self-consciousness had, as it were, been filled up with gestures. No obligation for the future lay in them, only the force of gravity on outward motions. And this had assumed the appearance of an artless inwardness in the small, narrow house of her mother. But now it was as though the breath was going out of her pliability.

She was sitting there quite helpless.

They were taking early coffee on the third morning. Her husband asked her,

"Well, Lorla, have you been in our drawing room then?"

"No."

"Y— — yes well — — why not then, eh?"

"Joseph, I don't like to ... a ... trust myself. It is exactly as if I were afraid."

"Why do you say 'were afraid'? Why not 'was afraid'? — You aren't at church or at school with the teacher."

"Yes, you see, it isn't right. That is, it's like if I say 'larf' instead of 'laugh!' Don't you sense that the house is like keeping its mouth shut?

Everything here at your place is too big, too cavernous, too high ... oh, I can't really explain it the way I mean it."

The coffee spoon which she was holding in her hand was trembling, she was so agitated by the words which were ringing out from her fear and helplessness. She looked steadfastly for a while in front of herself and when she then raised her eyes, the right eye remained pointing rigidly in a strange direction, only half closed by the weak eyelid.

"It would be exactly as if it were quite true what people say, that our house is haunted."

"Haunted ... oh now, not at all! But through the long, dark, hi—igh hall ..." she was subcon-

sciously stretching each word as though solemn-
ly singing.

"What, twaddle!"

"Twaddle?"

"Now, Lorla."

"Don't call me Lorla."

"Isn't it pretty?"

"Lore isn't pretty either. But 'Lorla'? No! Go
and say that to the doors out in the hallway.
Then you'll feel it yourself. — As if it's traipsing
in with wooden shoes ... yes, truly traipsing, it's
like that."

"Oh, Lore or Lorla, it's all the same."

"But if I ask you to?"

"Well, Jesus yes, for my part. Have me do
that. — Come, we shouldn't quarrel about things.
No! But because of that we can go see the
drawing rooms before I go to work."

She walked a few steps down the hallway in
front of him with her twitching patter and the
delicate mobility of her thin body. Suddenly she
paused and turned around.

"No, you go first, Joseph."

"The steps are wide enough for me to walk
beside you."

"No, you go ahead."

And she was already standing behind his
broad back which now pushed itself with the
steady gravity of short, fat legs in rotund, un-
ruffled rolling before her. Then he ascended the

stairs before her, jolting like a heavy burden. It was strange to her. She just kept her eyes on the large, imperious shadow of her husband and then on the thin, fluttering line which her body was throwing. It seemed incomprehensible to her how someone could move so steadily and surely in this large, austere, mysterious house. But she did not say anything because she was scared her husband would laugh at her or be indignant.

So the secret wonder stayed hidden within her.

They were then going from drawing room to drawing room. There were four, two connected by a broad doorway whose white paint already possessed the yellowed, quaint tone of age.

All the rooms were filled with furniture: large, showy, wide cabinets made from mahogany; low, long sofas upholstered in brown leather; stiff-backed settees with flowery, faded covers; tall and austere mirrors; long sideboards; round and square tables and desks; and beds whose feathered fullness reached halfway up the wall. Everywhere stood old pitchers, vases and glasses. Everything was more stockpiled than orderly, like in the warehouse of a furniture shop. Because of that, the abundance left a dull, heavy impression. The empty joy in possession had heaped everything up.

Leonore observed all these things shyly and when her husband paused with a look that demanded admiration, she would timidly feel the object with her fingers and whisper, "Oh!" — "But no!" — "No, no!"

The last drawing room was shut. When Joseph opened it, a musty haze, a heavy stale air came from it.

They both paused at the threshold, the cloth maker with a droll reverence on his fat face.

"Well?" he asked in aggrieved tone after a long silence.

"What is it!" Leonore began obediently, a little confused over this reproach.

"It dates from my great-grandfather in the sixteenth century. That was the same Liborius Griebel who built the house. He was alderman and in the end the mayor of Altenrode."

Leonore was now observing everything more rigorously. They were archaic, old pieces, badly riddled by worms; the covering on the sofa and chairs was extremely faded and chafed.

"The house has belonged to our family ever since."

"In the sixteenth century," Leonore said with a peculiarly deep tone and shook her blond head, full of wonder. She had only half heard her husband's words. The sound of her voice came from the expanse of her inner being, sent forth by a hidden sympathetic power. And the longer she looked at the old furniture the more everything became like a fairy tale which she had once known in early childhood and forgotten long, long ago ... long ago ...

"... long ago," her lips murmured in a low voice. Her husband thought it was an answer to his words, said a weighty "Yes!", closed the door again and led her out to the hall.

"Over there" — he pointed across the hall to a series of doors — "is the wool, the colours, the ingredients and the finished goods — come!"

"No, show me it another time!" she said petulantly.

They had walked down the hall and arrived at the stairway opening onto it. A dim shade flowed from it.

When Joseph tried to show her, she held back fearfully, "No, Joseph, no!"

"Now, come, childish girl. It won't bite you. I'm here with you."

"No, not today, another time."

"Well, at least just look in there."

And she took a quick glance in the half-darkness of the room.

"There you have in the boxes and chests enough rubbish that you could set up a flea market with it," he said smiling coaxingly and turned to go down.

But this tour was of no use to her either. She did not achieve control over her new situation. She was still frightened by the height and the opulence of the spaces; the straight, broad flights which spurned every trifling contact; the crowing, long echoes which every loud noise evoked and which then returned disturbingly to the most distant period of her inner being, but never petered out peacefully, instead they carried the agitation far into the expanses of her cramped soul.

And her unrest was growing. Her pattering became still shorter, her voice was deepening in its sound as though jammed.

"Mother, tell me what I should do," she asked distressed in the small, mean living room of her mother's house. "Everything in the Griebel house seems strange, big and wide. Even small things seem aloof. And when I'm thinking, it doesn't take long, it's not thinking anymore, no, it's like a gentle breeze playing with clouds in a blue sky."

"Yes, yes, girl, just like with us. Right isn't it, putting your hands in your lap and dreaming like a child. No, my love, there's nothing better in life. It compels with the broom, with the scouring cloth, swanning around in kitchen apron and skirts. — And I also want to say, don't spoil your husband. You must take him in your hands because it is fortunate that he has taken you, poor thing."

Leonore Griebel

Now Leonore suffused the house with her noisy industry and brought life into the quiet, austere rooms by her busy movements. She was striding through them with her outward force and penetrating pluckily into the most hidden corners. Thus everything became familiar to her by and by. Alone, when she was sitting quietly after her work was done, she had the feeling, however, as if she was only rushing quickly through everything and a deep dread overcame her that she was evading its inhibiting power. Escaping this motionless, strange prohibition, she drank the wonder of her own character in deep draughts. As though, freed from irksome constraints, something irresistible and yet with trembling timidity was wanting to grow out of her, quite, quite high and wide in wonderful colours, with surging, beautiful sounds.

Then she riveted her gaze tightly on the door which must soon open and let in something surprising.

In one such moment, a nursery rhyme suddenly occurred to her which she had learnt as a very small girl. She sang it with her thin, weak birdlike voice, still timidly to begin with, then deeper and fuller, right out of the depths of her soul, quavering for a long time at the end.

As long as the sound was quavering around her in the still air, it felt homelike. That blind, great force which seemed to stretch her apart inwardly returned by itself. A deep, mysterious pain was filling her which she could not defend herself against with the feverish stirring of her limbs, it was as though she was making the sensitive barrier which was inwardly rising against her dull, insensitive.

Her husband, however, saw in her struggling nothing but domestic industriousness. His stride became even easier and longer. He carried his head even more proudly and sat even more at ease in confident mastery.

In her helplessness, Leonore pressed closely by him, in the peaceful shadow of his broad existence.

The regular surges of his soul were flooding commandingly into her.

Her trembling body abjectly conceived its first fruit.

CHAPTER 6

Leonore Griebel

Leonore then lay like the linen in which she was lying, white and wilted, always in the weak trembling of her last breath. She did not at all demand to see the child. And when, after a few days, someone brought to her the big, strong boy, she gazed with large, astonished eyes at him and nodded silently. "I've called him August," the happy father said. "What hands he has! Look at them, and when he clenches his little hands. My God, he grips like a lumberjack."

"Away, take him away! — I can't listen! It's tearing me up!" Leonore cried out and shut her ears with the bedcovers.

Shaking her head, the nurse carried the child away.

Griebel, however, stroked her forehead,

"Yes, yes, sleep, Lorla, sleep and don't worry yourself. You will get your strength back before long."

She lay thus for weeks in her curtained room. She looked with large eyes at the ceiling and played with her thin fingers on the bed. Often quite quickly and trembling. Sometimes, while her index finger travelled with its nail slowly across the fabric, she seemed reflective. It made a fine, whispering singing sound. She listened to the steps of the people moving in the hall and was pleased to recognise them. The idle ticking of the clock in the upper hall, which answered back softly from all corners the often complete silence of the house with its articulated tones as though with sculpted lips, was cradling her in the safety of the restless forces acting around her. They were stirring, rising up from a distant impulse to be quite near her. They were then carelessly acting a play over her which was seemingly deaf and yet full of connections to her.

Then she shut her eyes and lay for a long time as though asleep. But the quick breaths and the hurried facial expressions indicated that she was inwardly engaged.

Griebel observed her often in such moments. When, in his view, her volatile rest was lasting too long, he would cough loudly or begin to stride about the room with heavy steps. Then she would open her eyes as though awakening and look strangely around the room.

"Where were you just then?" he once asked. She shook her head with smiling astonishment and shoved her white arm under it.

"Aah!" she said softly and stretched ... "a great, blue wall — oh! — from one mountain to the next, no, further, much further, was hanging over me. — — And as I looked up, you see, it stirred as if a wind was behind it. And then, quite slowly, it came down. It is already more as though it were wings, and I think, when the wings are already so beautiful, how must the angel really be that they belong to, and how I want to see, I torture myself, but ..."

"Oh no, look, you had your eyes shut fast, how could you want to see something?"

"Well precisely! For such a thing, I don't need eyes."

"Next, how did it go on then?"

"It didn't go on. You coughed then and it was gone."

— — —

"Sit up in bed."

She did so.

"Now, why then?" she asked and looked down at her bare arms.

"You have already been lying in bed for four weeks now."

"Four weeks ..." she said astonished.

"Aren't you sick of lying there?"

As an answer she just looked at him with large eyes.

After pondering for a while, she spoke with a misty-eyed voice,

"Oh no. — It's completely different now. — So peaceful in me, so far. Sometimes bright, some-times so dark. And beautiful things that I never *quite* see and hear happen there. — — — The funniest thing, however, is that I don't believe at all that little August is mine. It is all so aloof. Like in another life ..."

"But, think ..."

"No, listen to me. I *have* to tell you ... in another life ... yes, yes ... as if everything, everything! that had been needn't have been at all ..."

"Perhaps me — hey! — perhaps not me either?"

She drew a deep breath and looked at her finger whose play had already begun again.

"Dear!! — Perhaps not me either?"

"But Joseph!" she replied with plaintive voice, "don't be angry at the drop of a hat. Look, I can't help it. And who suffers more because of it?"

"I believe you, Lorla. I know ... well, don't cry. Look, I was just thinking. When I am out in the workplace, then everything here in the house goes all haywire. — I'm certainly not the Prince of Morocco either. Well. One is a cloth maker because of the money. And when nothing comes in, the mouth devours the body, as they say. Not so? — Do you see, I just thought that if you could get up and just see to things ..."

"You won't have me talked out of it. — — Oh yes! — — It's different a lot of the time too. — — When you go out so quickly and diligently, or when I hear barrels taken from the cellar and tapped, then I'm already up ten times and have started to make my bed because I want to see whether things are right, whether the chair has been carried away, that this and that has been done. But it just doesn't work at all. Not like I don't rise from bed or the chair, no. —

But look, when you do something then you first say within you, 'wait, it'll work now!' Then you set about it from the inside out as if you are agreeing with yourself internally. Then it works and you rejoice over it. — — — Isn't that so? —"

"Well ... hm, hm! ... I don't know ... oh, well some things ... it can be like that. I haven't thought about it before."

"And it fails me now. My arm isn't a man and neither's my leg."

"That may well be. I don't understand it. But I just thought that if you got up and tried out seeing to things. — Perhaps it'd be different if you were out of bed first. Just try! If it doesn't work, well it just doesn't work."

The next morning she really got up and put on the clothes which she had brought with her from her little house.

"This way everything will work snappily like at home, as if mother were standing behind me," she said to herself as she dressed.

Everything around her provoked her action. And she tackled it like an onerous reminder and cleaned it up immediately. But there was no plan to her work. She dusted the furniture, swept out the drawing rooms and then had to clean the dust off everything once more. In full swing, she noticed that the window panes were dirty. She called for water and cleaning rags. But without waiting for the execution of her instructions, she ran into the kitchen and began with the preparations for the midday meal.

"My God," she interrupted herself, "everything's still lying about up there in the drawing room. Go and carry some water in a pot, girl, I have to put things in order up there first." She stormed up there and began sweeping anew.

A strange force, her husband's will, was working in her and disorderly releasing the habitual grasp like the gears of machinery. Her industry was a confused fever. All the tasks huddled together in a mass. Her will was aimless, an anxiety which was driving her to act, to run with trembling hands, with shaking knees, gasping chest and glistening forehead.

Her faculty for action had really expired with the birth of her child. The strain of life to which her mother's energy had accustomed her had given way.

In the middle of the futile whirl of her work, she sank exhausted onto a chair and looked dully down at the floor to shrilly accuse herself,

"It's all still lying there and I'm sitting here!"

She sprang up and sank back down again.

"But I can't! — I *can't*! — It *isn't* working!! — My God, what should I do?"

With that she broke into tears despairingly.

She was experiencing the life in which she had given herself over to her husband's bidding like a constricting girdle. It was monotonous in its many-sidedness and yet confused and rough. The broad silkiness of her soul was wincing as though cramped under this merciless pressure.

She knew that the fulfillment of her work was her duty and yet was not capable of forcing her being to this bidding. With horror she felt it gliding away between the fingers of her will and she had the feeling of a growing liberation at the same time — for that which was swimming in the constricted expanse was herself, was that from which her true life drank its strength. But the anxiety which called after what was ebbing away with twitching, snivelling crying noises was dwelling there in the life of men which had always seemed so incomprehensible to her.

She felt with languorous pleasure, as her streaming anguish broke the strength of this anxiety, that the bidding was calling for her from ever greater distance, more and more muffled.

Like cast off, worked up, deep breaths, she was now enjoying the liberating weeping. Finally the last shadows of the present disappeared behind the horizon of her soul. Behind a soft veil, a gleaming, silent world was shimmering, with beautiful plains, quiet cities, gentle people without a care, and a sky which sang wonderful tunes with its changing colours.

The most discerning fabric of her organism thus magically transformed in the creative play of touch and flight the replica of the contentious, brutal world that her weak body had absorbed so infirmly, not yet broken and made enemies of by a strong instinct, not yet driven by emotion to a fervent demand.

In alert dreamy sleep, she enjoyed the tired, gentle wonder of inherited weakness.

Her elbows propped on her knees, her hands folded reverently, she sat there motionless in the middle of the drawing room. The broom lay next to her. With wide, shining eyes, she stared at the floor.

Then she heard the long, sturdy steps of her husband coming up the stairs, becoming harder and harder in the wide, echoing hall which the door opposite opened onto.

"Where is my wife then?" her husband asked.

"Yes, I don't know." It was the maid's voice.

"Is she up then?"

"Oh yes."

"And the meal? It's right on twelve."

"How can I finish everything if everything is left to me alone?"

Leonore would like to have stood up, but it was all the same to her, so unnecessary. She was not capable of breaking free from the force which was possessing her.

Her husband was already entering, coughing angrily, and his heavy work boots were treading even harder. He paused at the door, then he closed it slowly deliberating.

But Leonore still could not raise herself. Now it was a mixture of shame and defiance which held her motionless in her place.

"Well, how is it! — Is there no lunch today, hey?" he blurted out roughly, since his wife was not stirring.

Terrified she now jumped up. — No greeting and so hard? — And with her still dreamily gleaming eyes, which were anxiously beginning to tremble, she looked silently at him.

"What are you looking at me for? — If you're sick, get yourself to bed. If you are up, set to. That's how it is. I have to eat if I want to work."

With shaking hand, Leonore stroked the beautiful, soft hair from her forehead.

"But Joseph —"

"Oh now, I ..."

"You! ... You — ..."

The first time, she said the word like a reproach, then in teariness, half stifled by weeping.

"What, you don't what to threaten me with something?"

"Oh God, no, no! — I want nothing, nothing at all, at all, nothing at all like that."

Convulsed with weeping, she ran out.

After a short ponder, he hurried after her and called mutedly down the hall,

"Lorla, listen! — I brought something for you, something beautiful!"

But she was disappearing hastily up the stairs to the upper storey. About to hurry after her, he suddenly paused and shook his head, "No, Griebel, you won't do that!" Then he headed back hesitantly into the drawing room.

But it gave him no peace. After a few rounds of the room, he leant by the window, but soon stepped back hastily and began striding up and down the drawing room again.

"Hmhm — hmhm — — what — yes, I have to eat! — — — now! — — was I too angry? — Am I too much of a man? — — But she is still sick, since ... Why did she run out! She should surely have been pleased."

He pulled out a little red box and looked inside it.

Finally he overcame himself completely,

"Ah, I see how it is. I won't ruin myself just yet if I yield for once."

Then he climbed the stairs to the upper storey.

The door to the old drawing room was bolted from the inside.

"Lorla, silly woman, open up!"

There was no answer.

"Dear, I have brought something for you, something beautiful ... a ring."

The door remained locked.

"I'll be good again, quite, quite good."

No sound.

He deliberated for a while. Then he went back downstairs.

"Yes, I must simply have her busted out, hmhm! — But I would never have thought it of her ... and now already, now, after the first year!"

— — —

As he shook outside and a merciful tremor made his rich voice soulfully deep, Leonore tore her face from her hands. The door was vibrating! On tiptoe she hastened to it and tried to stop it. — No ... no ... oh ... no, never! ..." her thoughts groaned, and the wish radiated as a quite distant tone through their agitation that the shaking force was wanting to work up to an enormous power which would push in the door in insanely fevered ardency with its charge, smash the wall, trample everything, everything — everything — crowing to reach her leaning shaking against the door and clenching the lock with cold fingers.

The woman's instinct has awoken in her and she longs for a subjugating force which in incomprehensible ways must amount to her fulfillment and completion.

But he goes ... slowly ... without imprecation ... without pounding, without everything that hope allowed her. He goes with the customary, steady sounds of ease ... heavens! ... no! ... he even laughed??! ...

Blind, without sight, without thought, it tears open inside her and numbs her. Every cry dies in her and she sinks into the feeling of anguish, so strong in its dullness, of a woman experiencing her first disappointment.

CHAPTER 7

Leonore Griebel

But she is not a robust woman, she is a delicate spring flower which a propitious November has coaxed out of the feeble earth ...

She cannot wrestle herself into ferocity by the sudden emergence of a firm emotion. The splinters of her outraged soul are not yet yoked together into a carillon. It roars around her and in her with the shrill noise of an out of tune instrument: the shuddering of slack strings lurches into the singing vibrations of cloying melodies. This entire, silent world of beautiful plains, quiet cities, gentle people without a care, with a sky which sang wonderful tunes with its changing colours, is torn up under her husband's plump hand, desecrated and thrown apart.

She dispelled the feeling of being thrown out by everything ..., "... like a forest without end ... like an ocean ... an ocean, ... oh! — ... You? ... You? — — — if I ... ! — what then? — — — haha! — I ask all the world, what then? — God in blessed heaven, what — then?" —

It throws her further into pathless swirling vastness from turbid, agonising straits.

In between, the consciousness of a beautiful silence pulls on her with the stammering of a lost happiness.

This mad suffering lasts for a long, long time.
—

Then an inner stupor takes possession of her while her external senses enter a state of overly sensitive irritability. On the lower floor, the men are striding back and forth. Doors open and close. One is closed crashing; then a judder bounces all through the house. One is slammed heavily; then the great peace is startled with a grouchy moan, only to doze off angrily with obstinate grumbling when one of the big front doors goes swinging back and forth in its rusted hinges. Afterwards it is quite, quite soundless, and Leonore feels the silence flowing down around her with a strangely delicate trickling.

Only the clock is keeping watch beside her. And the streaming of deaf time sets its work into motion so that the pendulum cannot rest.

She is aware of it all, as if by chance contacts with the seam of her dress.

The light is coming diagonally through both windows of the old drawing room. In the dance of the light particles, the rising whorls of morning freshness are not pulsing. The tired circles of calming water are turning in the bronze tone of approaching evening. The long threads of the worn, large flowered sofa cover seem to be winding themselves confusedly in the evening light soundlessly like lazy worms. The heaps of dust on the worm-riddled furniture are also beginning to come alive.

The evening shadows glide from the ceiling further and further down the opposite wall. The weak light slowly creeps down to the floor, onto the one window and glides up a small table. Only the front legs can be seen, shadows hide the other pair. The front legs are trembling. It is as though the table is frightened by the night which is creeping up on it, and it is striving in fear to pull its legs up and bring them to safety. But it is not succeeding, and it is pulling a terrified face with its ornate seat. — At the same time, a delicate lamenting tone is becoming audible, a soft, soft whimpering, like quite small children beginning to cry. — Leonore's heart is palpitating. She stares rigidly at the table. Then she closes her eyes full of horror.

But the crying becomes stronger, is interrupted, and recommences again and again after short pauses with shrill screams. Then a sound is heard like that of a body falling heavily.

"Now the table has fallen over in fear," goes through her soul.

After a while, she opens her eyes timidly.

It is already quite dark. The table stands motionless as always in its spot, and it goes unnoticed that a trembling life has just resided in it's spiritless objectivity.

Relieved, Leonore breathes out.

But there! — — — It is still crying, hoarsely for pity and far, far away, like from another street.

She keeps listening for a while.

"It is probably little August?" And after that, "How far away it is, so far that it can hardly reach me." —

— "And yet I am his mother!"

Truly, and she cannot grasp it, this reality that seems impossible. Something is missing between her and the child. A space stands between them through which no feeling can make its way, a dead layer.

"The life that has died away with the child does that, the life where I could still work."

Now the crying was hoarser, quite weak.

She rose, "But that's no use at all, I am still his mother." With that she left the room.

Whilst she walked ever quicker downstairs, an image came to her: she was sitting as a quite small child alone in front of the house and playing. Suddenly she was afraid and began to cry bitterly. Then her mother came running to her, picked her up, and cuddled and kissed her in endless love.

And *she* was walking measuredly whilst her child was crying pitifully. What sort of mother was she? The knowledge of her wrong assaulted her with suffocating heat. She began running, fleeing, she hastily flung open the door to the nursery.

"Therese!"

Nobody was in the dark room in which the child was still weakly crying.

With hurried grasp, Leonore tore the child from the cradle and rocked it in her arms,

"Sleep, Gustav, sleep, sleep, sh, sh, sh …"

And while her tears ran down her cheeks, she covered his jiggling little head with trembling, hurried kisses. Oh, but only her lips were kissing, her demanding soul was not touched by the sweet, young life. That is why her crying turned to sobbing.

"Sleep! Dearest Gustav, dearest …"

Now she was hurling the words of love from her rigid fear. Fevered, she began walking.

But the interdiction of her cold powerlessness did not go away.

Exhausted, she sank into a chair which she had bumped into in the darkness. Her arms were trembling. Silent tears were running down her face, and all the time she was moving her lips quickly but mutely,

"My child — my child — my child …" in shaking helplessness and sorrow.

Finally the nurse barged in with lumbering steps,

"Now, who's the quick nanny then? — Oh, yes! Is it you, Mrs Griebel? — I ran down to the cellar for a tick to get milk. It didn't take any longer than it took me to count to thirty. — Well, then just give me the child again now.

Oh Holy Mother Anna! Mrs Griebel, you have such a face, pale as living death!?"

"Oh God ... oh God ... nothing more at all, at all, just nothing at all ... nothing! — ... anymore!" she murmured soundlessly and ran out the door.

CHAPTER 8

Leonore Griebel

Leonore was now lying all day long in bed again. She was also feeling physically wound up.

At first an impenetrable stuffiness weighed on her. With the exception of mealtimes, to which she took herself hastily and greedily, she lay there with eyes shut. The curtains were left shut for that reason. Then she was demanding fearfully for light.

The doctor felt her pulse and ran through the full scale of probing, tapping and conventional questions, then, entwining his hands behind his back, stood up by her bed in a thoughtful pose with his legs apart. After a while he shrugged his shoulders once and at the same time emitted a dismissive noise through his respectably large nose. Then he purred monotonously,

"Well, you stick prettily to bed for a few more days, eat regularly and then get up slowly. — There's nothing more. — Have a good morning, Mrs Griebel!"

He reached his hand out to her with his broad smile and strode briskly through the door which Joseph Griebel had opened for him.

"Won't you prescribe anything then, a little powder, pills, salve or something?" he asked when they had walked a few steps out into the hall.

"Well, Griebel, prescribe, hehehe! — Nothing wrong and prescribing! — Then, by all means if you want to dispose of your money, give me ten marks, that will help just as much."

"Jesus, don't scare me! Has it gone that far?"

"Yes, yes, that far ... You ... hehehe! ... I would have said something presently ... Your wife just has nerves, nothing else. — What do you want me to do? It will sort itself out again."

Then he offered the cloth maker his hand, simply nodded his farewell and went with his usual fugitive steps.

With an awkward jerk, he interrupted his haste going down the steps and returned to Griebel, "What I had presently forgotten," he began in a low voice when he was now standing close in front of the cloth maker again, "is very much something you could do, go easy on your wife for a longer time."

Then he left him again without waiting for an answer.

Leonore Griebel

Griebel remained standing in the hall for a long time without stirring, and stared with large expressionless eyes after the doctor.

"... well, ha! That is commonsense, he didn't need to say it. — Yes! — — nerves! — nerves! — — That doesn't please me at all," and he shook his head in sorrow disapprovingly.

Yes, if it had been backache, hot flushes, gout or something else, even influenza, "when it just goes no differently," a familiar illness so that you know where you are, but nerves, which a clever doctor can't get to work on! — Then a public prosecutor had leapt up in the middle of the session and had thrown himself out the window, a man in his best years — hmhm! — just for the sake of nerves, it had been in the newspaper — — — —

He crept quite cautiously back into the patient's room and sat down on her bed.

"Well hey, Lorla, how are you then?" he asked with a timid voice after he had been deliberating strenuously.

But the patient lay their with her eyes shut and did not stir.

"Is it sticking in your back? — Or is it pressing on your chest? — Show me your tongue! — Perhaps you have hot hands." — And he reached carefully for one of her white hands which lay slackly on the bedcovers.

Hermann Stehr

As he held it so gently for a while, he felt a slight trembling in it. It was becoming stronger and was making the hand's flesh limp and cold. He cautiously placed it back down again and then let out the breath that he had been holding.

He was feeling a peculiar embarrassment taking possession of him and it was pushing him to say something. He had to do it in any case. — Right! — The little red box which he had given her right on that morning after the execrable day was still lying there.

"Have you still not looked at the ring then, hey? — Don't you like it? — It is, I think, beautiful. It cost eight taler. See, if you hadn't run away, it wouldn't have seized you, Lorla! You will at least look at it!" And he held the open box out to her.

Leonore opened her eyes and looked at the red stone.

Then she emitted a short, strangely hard laugh. Nothing else.

"But Lorla, are you really still angry? — Look, it just makes you ill. — You must think of something else then."

Whilst he was talking, he caressed her forehead gently and lovingly.

Under this gentle gliding touch of his hand, her face turned red right up to her hair and her breath went ever slower and hotter.

Suddenly she tore his loving hand away with a hard push.

"Angry? — No — what do you mean? — I'm not angry at all."

With that she flashed her eyes cuttingly at him with gleaming severity.

Made quite helpless, Griebel went out.

When he was gone, the heavy stuffiness drained away from her in a few seconds.

She was in an ugly mood. She felt amidst longing a saturation, an urge to fight, so that she sprang onto her knees in bed, braced her arms stiffly and listened with flashing eyes to the echo of his steps walking away.

But this feverish pulling together of her character gradually sank back into the chaos of her inner being.

A break goes through all of us from the outset. In unease we strive for the clear possession of the world which suffuses us.

But in Leonore a fever had broken out, an attack.

The weary, sweet, gently toning paradise of her soul, that world which was composed partly from the reflections of forgotten fairy tales, partly from the ailing images which she had absorbed into herself from life, had seemingly vanished. She still felt in herself the mark of sainthood, but it did not open anymore to the endless expanses within her, nor into the deepest silence, not even in the wavering before her sleep anymore. And yet she had the unmistaken feeling of its possession. But a shadow stood before it's entrance.

This shadow dissipated in that moment of the feverishly-wavering pulling together of her person into a feeling of strength which she had never felt in her life before.

It was carrying out a regeneration in her — she was becoming a woman. She had been born as a child with dormant instincts. She had matured amidst the pangs of pregnancy. The chubby rawness of her husband had encountered her in the highest state of dream rapture and astonished her less than the birth of her sex's nature rashly called for.

Now a new body was forming in her body constantly critical moods, precise demands, fixed laws. All of this was so exclusively the outcome of an organic process that her consciousness wrestled with it in vain. She suffered under it in the beginning as though under an unpleasant change in temperature.

CHAPTER 9

Leonore Griebel

1

Now the bells with which she had been blessed were beginning to sound in her. But she did not hear them, for people only embrace clearly and intimately what they do not possess.

She had already not been suffering anymore for a long time.

But if you lie in bed for a long time then it is as if your innermost life is slowly detaching itself from the world around you and flowing into you, alone and orphaned as if in weary resignation. And the objects around you continue to live and every passing day gives them a new aspect of strangeness. In the end, you do not know at all anymore where they stand with their being.

This is the moment in which you experience the torment of your own life's incomprehensibility more oppressively than usual.

So it was for Leonore. An intractable, languid stupor in her ability to think was paralysing her as if a long vanished dream was working itself confusedly into her waking hours. Fluctuating sequences of images were stretching far into her deepest past, so that she did not know what was reality and what was illusion.

She did not understand why she married, how she had became a mother. An incomprehensible whirl had driven her through the house and finally thrown her into the bed. — That's why she was not moving from her bed, in the futile belief from somewhere that she had already experienced everything.

She had completely forfeited her childish talkativeness. She was filled by a dwelling suspicion. Even her mother learnt nothing of her state.

When the old woman came over after the closing up of her business and chattered sitting next to her, Leonore lay there quietly and pretended to listen to her. But she only saw the inextricable puzzle of her life, which with the closeness of this dearest person took on colours in which a mysterious possibility of understanding lay. At the same time, the dear intonation of the dry, motherly voice chimed over her rapt soul and thus magnified the illusion into a clear overview.

Once after she, lying on her right side, seemed to have been listening eagerly for a long time to

her mother's story, she asked with an impassioned jolt,

"How did you get to know my father then?"

"Now, tell me, how come you are asking me
that now?"

"Yes well ..."

She blushed and turned quickly towards the
wall.

Her mother said nothing fretfully for a while.
But then she asked with stilted voice,

"Hey, Joseph is good to you, isn't he?"

"What, Griebel?"

"No, Joseph, say Joseph with me. Griebel
sounds too strange."

"Well — — — oh I don't mind."

She was waiting patiently for the purification
of her inner state. She was often praying too.
But she no longer came thereby to the peaceful,
high expanses. As she was also striving for mind-
fulness, the prayer had become after a few
minutes an empty meditation which immediately
broke off abruptly and fervently when she heard
her husband's step in the hall. Then she covered
herself up to the neck and remained so with held
breath. A strange unrest filled her and everything
else seemed to be extinguished.

And if he then came to her with his long, slack
stride, settled down comfortably in the chair by

the bed and began to speak with the inevitable, "Well, Lorla, how are you doing?", she succumbed to an overwhelming disappointment.

She then laughed hard in the midst of his words or turned towards the wall in passionate haste and remained silent. And every time after that, the eternal question,

"Hey, Lorla, are you still angry?"

How she hated that!

But if her harshness had made him sad, she was sorry about it and she became talkative, often to suddenly break out again into a hearty laughter which she did not want to end at all.

"Haha! Joseph, haha, such a thing!"

She struggled against her laughter, and it whipped her for it, and then her cheerfulness always changed suddenly, became sharp, biting, scornful, until the tears entered her eyes. With convulsive sobbing, she finally threw herself on her face and dug her fingers deep into the pillows.

"Jesus Maria, Lorla, what's this about?"

He thought she would suffocate and wanted to tear her away. With fierce grasp, she pushed his hands from her body.

"Don't touch me, go!"

Then he left the room in deep chagrin and paused listening at the door for a long time in order to be at hand if a window rattled, for he could not get the public prosecutor out of his mind. But it always remained silent.

Leonore was kneeing in bed again as always, her arms braced stiffly. Her eyes flashed and her breath was hot and heavy. It was a consuming passion in her which she suffered under. She would have like far too much to wrestle with her husband. But he went away *again* with his long, gentle steps.

"Hm! — hm!!"

Her head sank onto her chest and she stared after him for a long time. She drilled her whole being into this gaze, which by and by made her drunk, dull, heavy.

Then she went to bed again and lay silently under the impenetrable burden of her life.

2

Tormented by impatience, she finally leapt from her bed at the crack of dawn and in the middle of fumbling for certainty.

"It has to come to an end."

How, she did not know, and what would happen was just as unclear to her. She was obeying the resolve of an emotion and it was transforming her. When her feet touched the floor, she was confident.

She immediately felt a bursting need to walk and took a few firm steps out of curiosity.

Nothing was hampering her as she did so. Her nightshirt just caressed the skin of her legs airily, gently, like a light, playful tickling, and she took a few more steps. With that an impregnable feeling of superior freedom came over her, a zest which seduced her into performing long, smooth movements as if someone was hidden nearby and eavesdropping on her.

She bent over to her left side. Then she quickly sprung her body up in the opposite direction, raised herself on her toes, rounded her arms over her head, let her upper body glide forward in a bow, shook the waves of her blond hair in firm refusal as though frightened by the speed of a grasp, recoiled with arms stretched forward repulsing and stood staring disappointed after the vanished for a while so — tensed, with faltering pulse and skipping heartbeat. — Then, with tingling light convulsions setting in, the game began anew for the invisible audience. It was a pacing dance, a silent mating call, and as the blood ran faster, hotter through her body, the idea of an eavesdropper became more definite, the contact between her and this mysterious being drew closer.

That excited her still more, and already she was beginning to hum softly and continued to during the process of dressing with the stranger.

Through an intermediate state, she saw him. He stood far-off, there where the possibility of dimension begins in us. His image grew from the simplest stirrings of space, from lines which recurred in everything, so simple that she saw him everywhere, that he watched from everything. In flight, on the waves of her easy movements, she glided before him.

The dawn brought her closer to him, the murkiness made him solider. In the increasing brightness, he was drawing away, more and more unreal. Only now and then did his image light up, lastly with the twitching play of simple lines ebbing away. A softer, more beautiful gleam at the edges of her soul was staring after the fading one frightened. Then it also sank like the dead light which resides in translucent, dry stems. With this it seemed to her as though she was wilting, collapsing, cooling down. Her enticing movements became wearier, more sober, heavier.

Now the first sharp ray was flying over the roof ridge of the house opposite and into the room.

Frightened she straightened up and stamped her foot angrily,

"Jesus, such an absurdity! Well, at least no one saw it."

Hermann Stehr

A humming sound of pleasure sounded from her husband's bed and interrupted her self-reproach so that she walked around concerned.

But Griebel just rolled his fat body over onto his other side. Then he began again his busy, regular breaths. The air streaming out swelled his lips a little each time so that the straight hairs of his thick moustache straightened out like a brush.

As she looked at him, a sharp anger arose in her, something like defiance. And, as a contrast, the mass of her finest faculties was weaving a countenance with other features around his face, in unreal breadth and only attainable by the eyes of her most hidden addictions. But the exhaled lines of his contours were becoming sharper and the picture which had just now been floating fluidly over Griebel's head sank over it and became solid: a pale countenance with a delicate, thin mouth. A ringing sourness lay over him which received a silent blessing through his high, white forehead. Over the large, deep-set eyeballs, white lids rested with thousands of deep blue, little veins. A restless tingling and trembling was running over his skin so that the long black eyelashes were constantly shaking gently.

Suddenly the cloth maker yawned loudly like the blast of a trombone and belted the covers in his sleep with his flat right hand.

Leonore was startled so that a chill ran up her spine. The strange picture was gone and Griebel's plump, good face with the long, fat cheeks, the hidden eyes and the oily complexion lay steadily snorting in the rumpled pillows.

"There he lies, hm, him!! ... and sleeps, haha!" With a jerk, she tore herself away and glided, imperiously upright and feeling a bitter coolness, past him and out the door.

The zest of the enticing dance gradually came over her again and brought her the deep inward satiation of a prayer. Made strong, she went along with it as though according to an enigmatic jurisdiction of her being.

3

The maid was stretching around in the kitchen, half dressed. When Leonore hurriedly entered, she started and stared at her in bewilderment for a while. Then she lapsed indifferently into her old pottering.

"When, dear, do you think we will be breakfasting?" Leonore asked excitedly.

"Dear?"

"Why me?"

"Well, Jesus, it's funny when you ask like that, dear!"

And she turned derisively towards the wall.

"I won't stand for that, you understand, Anna! — And stir your hands now and get a bit of a move on. My husband will be up soon."

She left the kitchen and looked to see if her husband was already up.

He was standing at the washstand and turning his large head with its disarranged hair. When the door opened, he stopped soaking.

"Well, off the feathers too, late riser?"

With that she disappeared again.

"Lorla! – Oh, Lorla! — At the first go ..."

He ran to the door and called her name into the hall once more — in vain.

"What is it now again?" And he stopped drying his face off.

"She creeps out in the night, makes over the house, runs like a weasel and lets the door fly. — And yesterday she still screamed when you merely offended her. — Hmhm!"

He shook his head thoughtfully and slapped the wet towel once over the back of the chair.

"— — whether it's really nerves, that's what I'd just like to know. As it seems to me to be that healthy and sick are all mixed up like cabbage and turnips. — — — Well, we'll see. — I'll with-stand it."

"Break—fa—ast!" her voice sings from outside.

"Well then, we have her back again already!"

He is quickly finished. Before going out, he pauses by the door as is his habit, stamps a few times hurriedly with his boots and at the same time shoves his trousers down still more with his hands. Then he straightens up slowly with evident strain,

"*Haah* — Well then, there!"

When he enters the sitting room, he finds the table already set. Everything is clean and shiny. A quietly pooling cosiness is shimmering over everything.

His wife is standing next to the laid table and gently sliding the pram forward with her left hand, while she adjusts the position of a knife next to a cup with her right.

"Well, a very good morning, Lorla!"

Leonore just nods and a soft redness rises in her face. Joseph has long since given up on the kiss. "The fuss doesn't suit a steady man anymore."

But oddly, his wife desires it today. And as she steps aside so that he can see the sleeping boy, she thinks of how at home she was always greeted by a kiss in the morning, "and that was just her mother". When he straightens up again, she instinctively looks at him questioningly.

But he does not understand her and begins with a good smile,

"Well, Lorla ..."

"... how are you doing then? — haha!" she finishes off derisively for that reason.

"Well, ha ..."

"... are you still angry!" likewise.

Disconcerted, he looks at her.

"She is still sick," he thinks and takes his place.

She sits opposite him, hands him sugar, milk and the bread rolls and at the same time says,

"See, I can parrot you quite well." With that she gives a ringing laugh which makes the sides of her delicate nose tremble.

"Right, Lorla, the fever has not yet gone entirely then?" he asks after a pause with stifled concern.

"Oh, pass me the bread and shut up," she replies laughing.

This cheerfulness is inexplicable to him and makes him more and more distressed.

Suddenly he stops eating,

"Well, but you were sick?!"

"We shouldn't get sick."

"What do you mean by that?"

"You are an old bear!!"

"Haha!" A wild mirth came over him and he drummed on the table with the index finger of his right hand. — "Haha ... then ... then ... tell ... me ... merely ... haha ... why then ..." He was speaking fitfully for laughing, but broke off abruptly when he looked at Leonore.

Leonore Griebel

She was sitting rigidly upright, pale, and the features of her delicate face were piercingly sharp.

He was suddenly frightened of having laughed, but pulled himself together and timidly put the question again,

"Why a bear then, hey?"

"Because you — hm — because with everything, but in everything, you so — so — so paw at it."

And when she had hurled that out in rising excitement, she held her breath. A desire to duck came over her, a fear of a sudden pounce. And in this fear, Leonore felt a strangely brimming abundance of strength.

But nothing happened. Griebel sat there for a while embarrassed. Then he softened his tone,

"Now you aren't simply angry again, Lorla!"

She received a dishonourable caning and her breathing became apprehensive and heavy.

The breakfast ended in silence.

Meanwhile Leonore succumbed again to her softness, and when Griebel made moves to rise, she hurried and grasped for his overcoat.

While she was taking the garment from the coat rack, her husband moved quite close to her,

"See, I knew it, Lorla, you are well."

His warm breath caressed her cheek.

Suddenly she had the physical feeling when he grasped her under the arms, gently teasing and yet with fingers whose trembling made a hot tingling run over her skin.

With a scream, she turned around,

"But Joseph, what are you doing!?"

"Well just, purely nothing at all. You can see, I'm just standing here. Why are you screaming?"

Truthfully, he stood there and gently stroked his long, fat cheek with the fingers of his right hand.

"Well yes. You are standing there like a ... God forgive me! — Here, take it!" she replied full of contempt, threw the overcoat into his arms and went out hotly.

"But if I know that it's just sickness," Griebel pondered behind her, assuring himself as well with a nod of the head, then looked at the boy once more and left the room ...

"... but one thing surprises me: that she does not look unwell, even if it weighs so much on her. No, on the contrary. She is becoming younger and younger as a result, it makes me say — — — but unaccountably."

He had stepped out the front door, had laid his right hand over his eyes and was looking up to the heavens. Then he walked curiously fast into the middle of the street, threw a searching look at the window of his sitting room and strode reassured on his way. In the process, he stopped off in his mother-in-law's shop,

"Good morning, mother!"

"A very good morning, dear mister son-in-law! — Well, what's Lorie up to?"

"That's why I've come over," and he explained everything, "Her illness has now turned her. Now she has hot nerves. That I'm not taking to. If you say to her, for example, 'Lorla, that is a bread roll,' merely the one. Then she stiffens, makes large, round eyes, waits a while and then screams, 'Then it is probably becoming ill.' Go see her. You will bear me out. And come over for a moment sometimes. We don't know what could come over her. Provided-for is better than thought-about."

4

On the most beautiful spring days, the laughing clarity of the young light suddenly turns without discernible cause into the impure whirling of the shimmering of a dusty breeze. You then view the entire world as if through fogged up windowpanes: everything looks softer, wearier, a quite gentle stirring of sorrow lies on everything, and the voices of sweet space sound muffled, from afar, timider, and the sobbing of people's talk sets in with an impassioned ardent frailty.

Leonore, who had alighted on a chair in her bedroom, was succumbing to precisely this change. All her certainty had become trembly, all that was bright had become vague, the clarity of her daily duties had become lawless. She was sitting as though shrouded in clouds. The long, measured step of her husband did not anger her. It still rang in her ears when he was already out of earshot and then lost itself in the hum of her own feelings like a muffled ringing. — She thus sat there, her hands in her lap and her fingers playing quickly around each other.

From time to time, she nodded slowly as if she now knew everything and, at the same time, her eyes became larger,

"Yes, yes ... life, life ... I don't know ... yes, yes! ..."

The entering nurse disturbed her.

"Where is Gustav?" she asked in her worn out manner.

"I'll stay with him. — Go into the kitchen and help Anna."

And barely had the nurse whirled out than the maid rumbled in with the question,

"Should I put on all the beef?"

"No, half of it. Take it apart by the big bone. Put the rest away for a roast."

Then she was alone again.

Outside the wind was sweeping through the street, the unruly wind of autumn. It was tearing the speech from people's lips and running away with it laughing. The groaning of overloaded wagons mingled with it in great delight so that it circled dancing behind the sides of houses and mimicked it. It threw the leaves and sand around and screamed uncivilised sounds into open doors.

The large Griebel house hummed in its noise and you did not know if it was out of anger or joy.

"It's going madly around," Leonore thought and rose to look at the boy.

But he slept soundly, his little fists pressed against his red cheeks.

She felt a joy at the sight, as though a soft veil lay soothingly over her entire body.

She pulled a chair over to the pram and reach-ed over to her knitting ... loop on loop leapt from the shiny needle — dreamlikc little circles which tauten noiselessly to an infinite chain in her: ... it is a beautiful hill in a blessed expanse. Desires were blossoming like silent flowers. The leaves of the trees were stirring gently. The golden light was dripping from them and placid brooks were drinking it with glittering eyes.

Once you heard a song behind the hill. It was there a long time.

Years later you return and sit and listen.

Everything is as ever.

Only the song is missing.

But you do not feel sad. For it rang for you once back there and still hangs silent with its nameless sweet motion in the air around you — over the silent blossoms — the gentle trees — the glittering eyes of the placid brooks — — — dreamlike little circles which tauten to an infinite chain in her: — — — and the boy sleeps soundly.

Then her mother arrived. Her eyes had the large, rigid look of worry.

Leonore rose, took a step toward her, kissed her silently on the forehead and laughed joyfully as if to say: don't worry. Then she flung her arms around her neck again in girlish charm. This embrace lasted a long time and her silent clasp had the temper of the revelation of a deep secret.

A waxen glow suddenly came over her and feverish kisses tumbled from her lips. In-between the shame of her avowals breathed, "Mother! — Mother! — Dear, adorable mother!"

When she finally wrestled herself off from her mother's neck, her glistening eyes were full of tears.

"No dear, Lorie! ..." the old woman was finally able to say.

"Oh Lorie! — Lorie! — Do you see, but he always just says Lor—la!"

"But it's the same."

"No, if it were the same, then, then … it'd be just the same, then …"

"Well now, such grimaces! — So that's it! — What have you done with him today!?"

"What?"

"Girl, don't pretend you don't know. He has … he is though …"

"He? — he!! — Of course. 'He' runs to mother-in-law like a boy, 'She's snatched my horsie.'"

"Now stop it! What do you want then? — Should he not go to mother, should he perhaps latch onto strangers, hey?"

"Oh!"

"That's right, that is no kind of wife. You were like an empty cake board and he had everything."

"But when I tell you he made me angry."

"How then? — Well, how then, has — No more of that! — Talk! — Yes, you see. Not a speck to it. Him, angering you? — My dear! A little water can't distress him!"

"Stop it, mother! It's becoming a performance. I don't understand it, keep it in mind, I just don't understand, I am entirely alone because I am his wife."

With those last words, she straightened up and a deep redness climbed in her face.

Her mother thought of the "hot nerves" and softened her tone.

Soon the conversation was gliding into that shallow, placid channel through which it is carried whenever women talk about everything.

Across from them, August awoke. Her mother immediately tore him from the pram and cradled him in her arms in tempestuous joy,

"The child will be hungry! — What joy he unlocks — ha! — slept in? — — — Like a Turk ... like a Turk ... wait ... wait ... for me, for me, little joy ... the boy is holding onto me so that he can unwrap himself."

"But not entirely unwrap, mother, he could catch a cold."

"Oh, it is warm in here though ... he must air himself a little here. — Just see there how he stretches, what a magnificent boy he is!"

"Jesus, but mother, what are you thinking?"

Leonore was glowing red and trying to cover his exposed lower body with a nappy.

"But girl, you are his mother!"

"No, that's not right, mother, no!"

"Now my God oh, you are married though now." And she forcefully pulled the nappy away again.

Then Leonore vacated the room, fleeing.

Her mother was baffled. Her face became deeply distressed. Slowly, like a laborious, heavy labour, she carried out the putting of the child to bed.

"Heaven knows what's with the girl. No, such a thing ... such a thing! — Yes, what would you think then. It doesn't fit in any trough in the world. What's the meaning of it then?"

She was still talking to herself when Leonore entered again with the nurse.

Old Mrs Marsel silently laid the boy in the nurse's arms, and when she offered her hand in parting to her daughter, she gave her a sign to come with her into the hall.

When they were standing outside, the old woman hastily grasped the young woman's hands and while she looked deep in her eyes, she said with hushed severity,

"Dear, sweet Lorie, pray, pray! — It is a quite wicked spot in which you stand now. Pray that you happily overcome it."

"Could be I can't, mother, can't; even if someone is there," she answered firmly.

The old woman left distressed.

Nevertheless Leonore was again in a little while in that calm, cautious mood, in the soft arms of an inner melody.

5

A soft, more hinted at, smile did not disappear from her face for a long time. She was also smiling with every movement of her body. She walked and worked in playful pliability, hovering, no longer in abrupt excitement, twitching. She adopted her own way of stroking her hair back at her temples. Then she slowly paused as though in the quiet certainty of an inwardly significant impulse, bent back her head as though drinking, and while she led the opposite hand in a broad arc to her forehead, in order to next pass raking through her golden locks over her narrow ears, she shut her eyes and her face took on a blissful expression. It strengthened and exhilarated her, the same as a profound quick prayer.

Meanwhile the maids' subordination under Leonore's clear will had also been accomplished, and so time was now breathing regular, seemingly gentle days through the large Griebel house.

Her hands on her back, her lips and head captured by the meanings of an overheard song, Leonore often strode back and forth in the hall for a long time.

It did her good to glide along the walls as the rolling folds of her dress excited the air around her. For she had the proud feeling then of a mysterious strength, an efficacy on the other side of the physical frontiers. The deeper her excited pacing led her into this feeling, the more animated arose in her a confusion of the deepest tones, the most burning colours, the most dazzling thoughts, the most abrupt moods, which were restlessly entangling each other in blind ardency.

All the strongest, devoted, saintly and pure lay in and ran through the air which her dress stirred up around her, and idly out from it without returning. And in this gap of her being by which everything melted away, the pulling of a longing then resided, a longing which was so agonising because no direction had dampened it yet. Thus she came to the conviction that she was living quite helplessly and in vain. Her heart bore out this thought in fervent pounding so that she stood still in fright and gazed into the hall with a questioning look. The vast, bleak calm did not take pity on her, but affirmed this apprehension with heartless silence.

Burning tears finally flooded Leonore's view, which was as deeply shocked as if someone had proved with a thousand good reasons the needlessness of her life.

"Oh you, my own God, where shall I go! — It's not my fault! — Why is it like this for me?" Then she hurried into the big garden and walked back and forth under the quiet trees, the urge of her

most distant soul calmed by the autumnal coro-
na of the cool-blue sky.

At this time, Griebel sometimes came into the
garden too. While she was strolling under the
trees, he crept around, amassing wizened little
branches, here and there cutting off a reed,
binding a loose sapling firmer, then turned quite
abruptly to his wife,

"Lorla! Hey, beautiful weather isn't it, don't
you think? — Well yes, yes. We've also had it
otherwise. Thundery and grungy, a loathsome
rain and day after day of muck. But it's beautiful
now, that is true!"

He talked like that or similar, without inward
concern. At the start of his words, he straightened up as though to say something important. But
he was already scattering the last words again,
partly mumbling, partly shouting needlessly,
alongside his tinkering and raking. Leonore let
him do as he liked, smiling. — When he stepped
alongside her once and, holding the same pace,
wanted to stroll around with her, she gave the
appearance to start with that she did not see
him. But then she turned to him, stopping, and
appraised him in astonishment,

"Are you serious?"

"Yes — dear God, serious? — How do you
mean? — Serious, no, more for my pleasure."

"You want to speak of pleasure. Does such a
thing really give you pleasure, Joseph?"

A pleasant surprise made Leonore affectionate.

"Oh, well admittedly, once, twice around the
garden you can bear. But as a habit? No! For I
will tell you something — but don't pull an ugly
face — a man is simply different from a woman,
we like to say: like winter weights of wool and
beautiful, smooth fine wool, it is ..."

Leonore angrily interrupted his convoluted
line of reasoning.

"Oh now, don't bother, Jesus Maria, just don't
bother if you don't enjoy it! Who's forcing you to
then? — I won't take offense. Go from me and
continue your fumbling around in the garden."

The doctor had recently advised him to let her
have her way in everything so that she could
continue to strengthen her nerves. He thought of
that and immediately began his old occupation
obediently again, since his conversation had not
found her acclaim.

Leonore actually seemed hardly touched by
the apathy of her husband. She strolled to the
other end of the garden, hovering as though
levitated by the limpid light which was playing
around her, and she drank the beautiful calm of
the fruit-laden, autumnal expanse hastier, for
her husband's behaviour had strengthened the
drawing longing which resided in the gap in her
being.

On a walk with her husband, this drawing longing became an image of her most hidden soul. It was on one of those wonderful late autumn days which divulge all the nearby wonders in shimmering, three-dimensional clarity to us.

They were strolling on a little-used cart track which slowly climbed up the long ridge of a hill dividing two valleys. They were deeply cut mountain valleys and a bustling village lay in each. Both valleys lost themselves in forests winding toward the distant high ranges. There factory chimneys then peeked out and the slow groaning of the ironworks poured idly through the village lanes. It sounded as though a weary giant was telling a long story, ejecting each syllable of his monotonous words always with the same, rough force. The pauses in which the little peacock of exhaled steam became audible like heavy breathing filled the monotonous village life with gentle chatter.

The cloth maker and his wife strolled into the field as they leisurely followed the climbing windings of the solitary path. The sound of their footsteps was becoming softer and softer. It now sounded just like a gentle booming which was integrating in regular beats with the vaguer pounding works in the distance.

The quiet gravity of the autumn light was swaying in the delicate wings of a soft breeze to those long, sharp tones as can only be sung by October's wind with gently wrinkled, musing lips. The ploughed fields played around them with the glory of future fertility. Swarms of birds were throwing themselves in darting lines from bush to bush like skittish, turbid designs of heaven. Larks were running busily in the furrows, then stopping behind clods of earth and stammering a few timid trills with an abrupt, snivelling break. But in the high heaven, mountainous clouds were strolling in silent majesty over the blue chasm, driven by a hidden, inaccessible power — a silent, gigantic confused surging — a battle whose violence looked like shadow play. For the storm of that struggle was still far-off, so far away that its sounds could not reach the earth.

The latter was lying in the undisturbed dream of a day whose ever present light was grasping with its deepest, trembling life after the great background, those weather conditions remote from the world.

A rising hastiness was coming over Leonore. She hurried to the peak of the ridge. And when she was standing there, she drank the sky's silent cloud-battle with wide eyes. With that a feeling of intoxication took possession of her, which she thought she could escape by laying her hand over her eyes.

When she thus stood there, looking into the self-induced night, a rising general uncertainty awakened in her. The ever narrowing circling waves of her passion, excited by the events taking place, were thrusting her own image into her consciousness.

Meanwhile her husband had joined her.

"Why are you keeping your eyes shut?"

"... oh — quite far away ... far away ... it swims in it ... lost and forgotten as though one were nothing ... but it flourishes green and blue, you hear singing ... thunder! Like shrubs! ... You want to be happy and are afraid. — Blessed heaven, now it's as if something shiny is coming and fetching me and carrying me and swinging me, far away over all the mountains ..."

She was speaking quietly, enraptured, with a passionate flooding in her voice,

"Dammit! Now take your hands away and stop that prattle! If someone came, they'd think you were a bit funny in the head," Griebel interrupted her irately.

Leonore opened her eyes and laughed happily, "Then I'm with you again, you, dear, haha! dear husband. — Oh, but it was far away! — Close your eyes please, now!"

Griebel squeezed his eyes shut so that they looked like bulging fissures. And wanting to be certain of the closure, he screwed his corpulent nose up in fat folds. He remained thus for a while and waited for an epiphany.

"Well, what do you see then?" Leonore asked impatiently.

"Nothing!" he snorted laughing and rubbed his opened eyes. "Childish stupidity!"

6

Leonore thus entered a dream state again. It differed from the constant mysticism which had earlier filled her soul by the forceful play of an episode. It blossomed into the noise of day. In the midst of work, she succumbed to it, to a soft, dissolving languor. Then she felt it blossoming as it stretched the withered passages in her through a flood of fertilisation breaking forth. And she became addicted to these moments without reproach. With no tearing of the will towards duty like before, she rattled at the doors of her consciousness. Thus the primordial division of her being was disappearing. Her day strolled into her dream, and the pulse of her soul pounded in every grasp.

Then she sat, seemingly as always, moving her thin fingers in uneasy play. But her pale blue eyes did not stay lost in a keen face, rather her face glowed and her chest beat fiercer, a victorious trait lay in her flourishing countenance.

For her figure was rounding out more and more. The germinating swell of a young bosom was blossoming in fuller flushes. The whites of her nails gave way to an ever fuller red, and the tired blond of her hair turned golden.

The empty song of her soul also seemed hushed. The morbid rigidity had gone from her right eye. If the lid also still lay over it in its old weakness, then it was moving under it without inhibition like the star of the other eye. She often also felt a namelessly sweet, hot fullness when she kissed her boy.

Abruptly boiling fervour then tore her from the path of her usual work. She threw away what she held in her hand, hurried fleeing to the child and took it jubilantly from the cradle.

“Mrs Griebel, you don't have to always tear Gustav from his sleep. And if you will anyway, then nice and slow. — So he wakes up slowly. He could get spasms from fright one day,” the nurse pointed out to her.

It was the heaving of fervent blows, like when a storm arrives.

Then the old strangeness, the dead layer, again lay for days between her and the boy. In vain he reached for her with slurring noises from the nurse's arms. She walked past heedlessly, hardly throwing him a distracted, empty smile, and his crying did not stir her nature.

Even in the midst of the whirl of her fervour, she succumbed to this icy disconnection.

The boy's movements, which were still surrounded by a shimmer, were becoming repugnant to her. The aroma of sweet childhood was disappearing and she was smelling the sweet-and-sour stuffiness which simply lies around small ones. The blissful music of children's voices which only the heart hears seemed to have fallen away, and she was hearing intolerably piercing noises.

Then she flung the boy down and hurried out to sit for hours in a daze which merged in the end into a rapt stupor. She avoided all society and walked about disturbed until a gentle weeping finally delivered her from the clasp of this emotional paroxysm.

In calm minutes of clear consciousness, she made up her mind firmly to counter these fervent attacks of her "mood" by a constant sweet temper. But what did the cases in which this self-compulsion succeeded count for against those common outbreaks which forced her to push her child away in painful distress!

"Why are you casting Gustav aside again like a changeling?" her mother asked her, as Joseph had brought Leonore's "new illness" to her attention and she had come "to set her head right" again.

Leonore had fled to the window and was staring out blankly. She did not answer her mother's question because the exhaustion of her disillusionment had left her unmoved.

But her mother did not rest from agitating with questions at the door of this puzzling condition. For a long time it was in vain. Leonore finally turned around and looked deeply at her with a bitter gaze. Then she clasped her hands between her knees and moved her upper body trembling back and forth.

"Hm, hm," her voice added trembling, "what should I say first? It's just something again that you won't understand."

"Dear Lorie, look, I'm your mother, and I'm distressed when you treat your child like that. I can imagine it hurts your own heart! No? — Don't cry, Lorie, better you tell me! Perhaps I can help you."

Leonore shook her head sadly.

After a while of seemingly weighing it up, she explained it with that breathless cadence that incomprehensibly sad fairy tales are told in,

"... there is something about the child that is more beautiful like flowers in the light, like singing birds ... something. It comes and goes without me calling it or driving it away. It blooms from the child and sinks back again ... and yet there isn't a breath ... another life from the living ... Jesus, how can I just say it! — Yes, see, now I have it ... when it's night and the moon is shining. You walk ... by the mill stream and look over the meadow. The grass is black as a pond and the water moves like a dying man. Then you walk quicker and look around. Over there, in the middle of the meadow, an angel is standing in white clothes and waving at you with its arms, and its brilliant wings are fluttering. You cannot help yourself and fear and joy is like an arm pushing you. But as you come nearer, the beauty blurs more and more. Now you are finally there and stretching your hand out to it ... then you are grasping a thorn bush so that your hand bleeds. It is rustling around you, and everything is ugly and empty so that you become fearful and frightened. — See, mother, that's how it often is with my child ..."

Her story tailed off joltingly into an excited dreaminess. She rose and looked down before her. Then she stroked the hair on her left temple back with her right hand. With closed eyes, she stood there leaning back.

Suddenly she stopped cuddling her body in the shock of an abrupt realisation.

"... yes, truly ... as if it wasn't my child, that I liked having, not taking out, not holding, not kissing, no, the other one, what is up with him ...

the other one ...! But tell me, where does the other one come from?"

She let her arm drop limply and stared at the curve of its fall.

"Did you see my arm dropping?" she said after a few moments and looked at her mother with large eyes.

"Oh, now indeed. — There is just nothing further to it."

"No? — Right. It's just confusing and it seemed to me then as I saw my arm falling as if it could be the answer to my question."

7

Human life has days like the time out of which it grows, a wonder of the world.

The days of human life also climb from nights across the visionary bridge of dawn. In those early hours of the soul, since it plays with the intimations of its fate like the earth with climbing mountain haze or clouds coming down, the deepest songs of eternity are deceived by the division of the senses from the infinite — — —

The break of day ...

In that early morning in which impatience of waiting drove Leonore to bed, the laws which eternally governed women became flesh in her.

Before the invisible redeemer of her fate, she had danced enticingly. The soft curves of her motions, the quite discreetly sweet concert of her physicality had inducted her into the inner court-yard of love. And then her dream was singing this same music in enraptured flushes with soft ghost-lips into the sound of her day and of her tremulously begging yearning in which she was blossoming trembling, a wonder in a wonder.

More and more her condition merged together for support in that fervent disorder-liness which belongs to weak natures.

Unconsciously, her unsatisfied soul was drawing the content of her entire past to a jolt. Quietly, without overview, in slow inexorability, every eye was turning blind to her nameless hopes. Only one eye remained open. Its vision exhausted her completely so that nothing was living outside her anymore.

The bright bell peels of a sledge gliding past unleashed her hunger for a sudden intoxication which she relished in anticipation as though a rushing curve was travelling through her and its movements bringing a hot rapture over her body and thoughts.

Then she began singing overrunning, never heard before melodies on "la". In heart-pounding jubilation, she sang with outspread arms, wandering back and forth in flittering steps. It was as if she was dropping an anchor with this strange song.

From these wings of endlessness, she was plunged abruptly, like with a broken swing, into the clatter of the everyday. And when she, struggling for understanding, looked around herself in the familiar rooms, strange tears shot into her eyes, such tears as those attacking her eyelids acridly with seething poison and running burning down her cheeks.

"What are you crying for, Lorla?" Griebel then asked her.

"Hm!" and she looked cuttingly at him, "hm and are *you* still asking that, *you*? — Oh you, my dear God."

And she threw herself down on her knees next to the chair she had been sitting on and beat her clasped hands on the seat as though dazed. For her body's beautiful strength had become even fuller. The surges of her blood were going higher. They were not sowing dreamy colours and pictures in the crop furrows of her inner world anymore; they were tearing screams out, glowing red-hot, warping her inner being's secret instrument so that its strings made disorderly vibrations. Everything then seemed to her to be lost and she cowered there in the dullness of shock. She felt as though shrivelled to a point.

A force over which she had no control was throwing her from agonising jubilation into a turbid fear. Her passion was lacking the power of distraction, the sound reserve of a conventional life in which her soul could rest like the petrel on the sand bank.

She was as though naked. Nothing pursued her into the fervour. She was being led further and further from everything and everyone about her. She fled before the kindhearted, earthy words of her mother, whose love knew only the blows in her wounds. But her eyes always returned alone from that puzzling shore of her innermost soul. She always found herself again on the path from the kitchen to the sitting room, in the loft, in the old room and yet she never encountered her home in her house.

And she never congealed into the glow or the rapture of dullness. She was not strong enough and not weak enough for madness.

8

Thus she gradually headed into an ever increasing predicament.

She often sat there in a purely physical wavering, completely enraptured and exhausted by this lustful state. It even ambushed her whilst walking. When she then stepped onto the street, the grey, bland house fronts obtained a beautiful finery. Their panes shimmered. The people went in and out as though dancing. And they listened rapt to every word they said, for everyone carried the traits of goodness and friendliness.

A maid with a red, laughing face like her, carrying a basket on her arm, was skipping across the street and humming a tune through her teeth.

Leonore felt such a strong bond to the unfamiliar girl that she shouted to her, quickening her step.

The girl stopped, nodded amiably and asked,

"Well, good morning, Mrs Griebel?!"

"Oh is it you, Pauline von Heinzeln?"

"Yes, yes, do you know me too?"

"Oh now indeed, I'm too good to you."

The girl blushed and fell silent. The she said quite timidly,

"I must, however, move on now, otherwise my lady will grumble. Adieu, Mrs Griebel."

"Adieu, Pauline, but do keep singing, sing!" Leonore called after her and watched her full of happy feelings, through whose light, wistfulness was drawing like threads of mist blowing away. Never such a young, cheery maid, oh my never, never, that is surely something beautiful, she thought to herself.

Another time she came from the Ring and was strolling down the broad Kirchstraße. A biting north wind was boring down the street. For that reason she kept to the left side footpath. When she had arrived at the cooper Meergans' where the narrow, dark Wassergasse ran into it, she steered her gaze into it. The lane looked just like a half-dark gorge because the wind in whose direction it lay skewed was blowing the snow in it away in clouds with restive, driving churning. An icy powder was getting into her eyes so that she had to close them. After a few moments, when she could raise her eyelids again because the wind gusts were over, she saw a lovely image. A boy of about five years, wrapped in all kinds of cloth so that he looked like a bundle, was leading a smaller girl by the hand. He was carrying something tied up in a red handkerchief and watching his companion anxiously as he lead her to-and-fro so that her little feet would not step into snow that was too deep. As soon as a new wind gust announced itself with high howling tone from the eaves, the little boy laid his pack down on the ground and entwined both his arms around the little girl to protect her from being blown over. It was a cheer to both of them. She squealed a happy laugh in the noise and when the danger was past, she flung her arms around his neck and kissed him many times. Leonore's heart beat in joyful surprise so that she could not move.

The cooper stepped out of his house.

"Good morning, Mrs Griebel! Aren't the little mushrooms like a pair of lovers. The little boy does it much better than his elders. It's the gas man Schneider's boy and the smith's Lenlein." Leonore smiled distractedly and then walked on with cautious steps. She kept close to the houses and her right hand grasped the wall haltingly, as she was reeling and continually murmuring to herself enraptured,

"They kiss each other ... as they kiss each other ... they kiss each other so beautifully ... they kiss each other far too beautifully ..." Then she was reading all the signboards. They seemed to have a wonderful significance. "Johann Laufer, rope maker. Karl Nieder, Good Sauerkraut, Rustic Bread, Herrings," and she did not believe these everyday words and yet could not find the cheer and bounty which glowed behind any of them either.

Near the street corner, she had the feeling that she would hug someone who was there on earth coming from the other side and call him sweetheart. For that reason, she slowed her steps to not collide with him. But most people walked past indifferently. Some certainly greeted her amiably and acquaintances pressed her hand heartily. But none of that was the beautiful and pleasing which had waited around the corner for her. So Leonore's eyes all went blind bit by bit — only one remained open.

On an afternoon around four o'clock, she tore the kitchen door open, ran into the middle of the room and looked around questioningly. Her eyes were wide open from fervent expectation and her cheeks were glowing.

"What are you looking for?" asked Anna, who was just placing crockery in the cupboard, and looked over the shoulder at her mistress.

"Well, I just heard it though."

"What then?"

"It must have come into here."

"Oh, the clock is ticking, nothing else."

"I heard it. Someone opened the door, came up the steps, stopped at the top for a bit as if considering, and then walked with long, easy strides …"

"Well, — long, easy — I'd like to uncover who — long, easy … haha! — Anna went into the hall barefoot."

"No, it was a man!"

"Well, Mrs Griebel, now calm down. I understand now what you're after! A man? Hey? A man? What? — I don't have a sweetheart and not even in the light of day. I couldn't stand one!"

"But, Anna, such a thing. Who's talking about a sweetheart, such a thing? — Shame on you!"

And, while Leonore was stammering the words, it seemed to her as if she would fall over, her blood was roaring so much. She could not look at Anna for shame and fled from the kitchen.

"Who should be ashamed?" the disputatious maid cried, emboldened by her flight, "Me? I didn't hear any man, I didn't ..."

Suddenly she broke off and let the right fist fall which she had been shaking at the closed door. Then she stared in front of her with an expression which changed slowly from fright to scorn.

"Oh, like that?" she murmured at the same time. "Well then, why couldn't that be the case! Her husband is really just an old feed trough and she is still just a girl, nimble, pretty, appetising ... yes, anything is possible. Well, I will be paying attention."

She heard the sitting room door opposite open and went quickly to the cupboard because she assumed Leonore would be coming to take her to task for her last, meaningful words.

But the door simply shut again soon afterwards and everything remained quiet.

Leonore had fled from the kitchen and fallen in the sitting room with her face against the seat of the sofa. Her body was swelling and shrinking under her heaving breath. It filled and emptied itself shaking like an over-divided, numbed tube through which the blasts of a wild fan were being driven.

And she felt streams of fire coming from her closed eyes so that her eyeballs burned like glowing coals.

At the same time she was murmuring in fervent confusion,

"Who can say I have a sweetheart — me? — me have a sweetheart — a sweetheart? — sweetheart? — sweetheart?"

Her breath blowing back struck her face searingly. It was as if a sweet fragrance was residing in it, and she kept murmuring the wonderful word, ever quieter, sweeter, more intimately and drank the fragrance, filling her breath with it. Her trembling bosom was drinking it, her longing soul, her whole feverishly blossoming body.

Finally she rose and sank onto a chair in a fluster. She sat with closed eyes, her head slung back, and her shaking right hand stroked her forehead with gentle fingers across to her left temple.

Her soul was like a summer field over whose blazing flowers the light of the midday sun burns in glimmering fervour all the way to the blurring horizon. Her gaze was singed from within, and when she opened her eyes, she looked at every object through a grey veil with flowing contours, floating back and forth, surrounded by a pale shimmer. Suddenly it came over her like the lust of conception: movements from and around her flowed together; a body released itself from her body; her face became her countenance; a beam came out of her eye and estranged itself, and a being came into existence.

Still she did not see it, but felt its good, encompassing gaze directed at her. From there in the corner next to the cupboard. Drinking it with her body, she sat and dared not look up for humble joy.

A soft gliding finally made her turn her head. But she could not distinguish anything clearly. Only when her pounding, labouring heart ejected a new stream of blood did the outline of a masculine being begin to appear more distinctly out of the dim corner next to the wardrobe, where the coat rack was on which a man's overcoat and hat hung. Moments later deep breaths were also raising his body from the void. But when she composed a piercing glance to get some certainty, she felt it in her inner being like the abrupt collapse of a beautiful world. The great blossoming field of her soul was disappearing behind the narrow cupboard of her consciousness, and the objects surrounding her were fading into the usual outlines.

"Well, sweetheart, where are you?" Leonore asked with bitter scorn and yet could not stop the wistfulness residing in the emptiness of her words. She rose and strode through the room to collect herself. Every item she came across, she touched with her hand. At the same time, she said mutely,

"Here a chair — the table — the sewing table — the linen cupboard — another chair — — — always so, the same today ... tomorrow ... in a month ... in a year — until I die —"

Suddenly she collapsed at the table on which she had been leaning on during those last words, threw her hand-entwined arms stiffly over it and let her head sink under the tabletop.

She remained like that, as though lifeless.

The empty winter evening let its misty detritus trickle down ever thicker on the windows.

When she heard her husband's step, she sprang up terrified.

"What must he think, that I still have no light on?" The words passed through her head with the keenness of an uneasy conscience. And while she was searching ever more fearfully in the sitting room for matchsticks, she heard her husband open the kitchen door and ask inside,

"Is my wife not here?"

"Oh yes!" answered Anna.

"Well, it's dark though in the sitting room."

"No, she hasn't gone out. Definitely not. A short while ago, it was afternoon, she came into the kitchen and asked after a man."

Leonore stiffened with terror when she heard these words from the maid. She had to hold onto the windowsill. At the same time she grasped the box of matches.

In an instance there was light.

Her husband also entered then.

"Good evening!" he greeted her upset and hung his hat on the coat rack. "Well, where have you got the man?"

"Me? What, a man?"

"Well, Anna said you were looking for a man?"

"Anna, *her!* does she want to bring some strife into the house? Isn't it enough that she is as coarse as whole grains! She must leave the house now. Should I perhaps follow, am I mistress or servant?"

"Now you're starting with me and making my head full. Bothers everywhere, at work and at home!"

"Can I help it when you start grumbling before you've said good evening?"

"Jesus, Lorla, it isn't worth the bother or the worry. Can't I have a bit of fun!"

He grasped teasingly at her, but she eluded him and left the room aggrieved.

When Anna had then served the evening meal and was wanting to leave the room, Leonore began again obstinately,

"Stay here please, Anna! — Now please tell my husband, was I looking for a man?"

"A man? — Of course, you asked whether he was in the kitchen."

"Whom would I have asked about then, if it were true?"

"I don't know who you were after, that you'd probably know better. I, for my part, I don't have a sweetheart," the girl replied crudely and left the room.

Leonore threw her hands before her face to hide her shameful blush from her husband, and broke out into tears.

"There you have it!" she cried sobbing. "She knows absolutely nothing and speaks of a man, a sweetheart even. Have I once lied to you?"

"Now, Lorla, you know well that Anna has a dense head. But she doesn't mean it like that. Now stop your crying and tell me rather how it's been."

Through affectionate coaxing, he finally calmed her down so that she told him the facts. Of the state of her inner being, he learnt nothing, for it was a secret even to Leonore.

When she had finished, he shook his head and said with a condescending smile,

"Jesus, yes, everyone mishears once in a while. There's no need to make such a fuss. It was probably that a man was there. That is, the traveller from Frankfurt who pulled a fast one on me last year with the indigo wanted to come.

— — But now, forget it, we will see what the crude devil, Anna, has cooked."

Then he made himself comfortable at the table with long-winded sociability.

While he helped himself attentively and with enthusiasm, Leonore sat forlornly there and barely touched a thing. Suddenly she laid the hefty knife and fork down and said a repudiating "No!"

"Well?" Griebel asked without looking up.

"Can you hit me, just from anger?"

Griebel let the hand sink with which he was just wanting to lead a piece of sausage to his mouth, and looked astonished at his wife. "You have had one of your bad days again today," he thought. Then he answered,

"Lorla, silly girl, such a question!"

"No, you should say: yes or no."

"Well, if you want to know: no."

"I thought so. — Now continue eating!" She said it with a dismissive, bitter smile and ground a piece of bread into crumbs at the same time. Then she looked for a long time at the window behind which the wall of dark night was standing, and she did so with impassioned eyes.

Griebel "grazed" and prattled in a mixed-up way at the same time.

Leonore suffered from the large hole in her life. Her soul lay by distant shores and struggled and cried and prayed and despaired. As a result the colour of her face became paler and paler, her body's pose more and more rigid.

The "yes" and "no", which she strewed in often unsuitable places in the chatter of her man, bore the colour of her innermost being: they sounded hesitant, begging, trembling, aching just like the whispering of the lost.

It became more and more uncomfortable for Griebel at the same time. He talked with ever longer pauses and finally kept silent unsettled.

Then it was deathly quiet.

And the souls of both persons suffered under it in silent horror.

Leonore came back into her life first, and still standing under the interdiction of her fate, she said mutely and keenly serious,

"You're sitting far from me — far!"

Griebel was startled by the thoughtful eyes of his wife, and while he scratched at a mark on his vest, he said uncertainly,

"Yes, yes, it is funny sometimes how our eyes deceive us. I could tell you such a funny story too. — But let's leave it! I'm tired today."

Then they both rose and made arrangements to go to bed.

Leonore broke off and asked him timidly,

"Does the traveller also go to sea?"

"The one from Frankfurt?" came Griebel's bored counter-question. At the same time he scratched his head.

"Not him alone. Men in general."

"Oh now indeed, such have most enough who come here."

"It is deep — and – wide ..."

"Now then, Lorla! I tell you, nothing like sky and water. The ships come and go, and no one knows if they'll see the people again who go on the ships."

With that he blew the lamp out and they made their ways to bed.

For a period, Griebel listened uneasily to his wife's breathing which went short and heavy.

"If she could just sleep well. Then it'll all be well again tomorrow," he pondered. Suddenly the agonising certainty ambushed him that his wife was kneeling in bed and ringing her hands despairingly over her head.

He lowered his voice and asked seemingly indifferently,

"Are you lying down, Lorla?"

But the answer was not forthcoming.

For that reason, he called louder,

"Lorla!"

"Yes," she answered swimmingly weak.

"What are you doing?"

"I'm thinking about the sea. Some like to sail it because no one stops them. But when they are out on it and have just the Lord and water around, then it comes over them that no one is looking after them. A single good heart would have stopped them. But now they are sailing out into the unknown and are afraid in their souls."

Griebel was unable to answer. The great, empty silence which had divided them the entire evening was becoming stronger between them.

The monotonous noise of the sleeping house flowed into it. It sounded like the gentle waves of a distant water.

CHAPTER 10

Leonore Griebel

For a long time, a quiet calm lay over Leonore, like the resignation of the knowing who have learnt to be humble. But it was only her tiredness which looked like that. Her pilgrimage to innermost happiness was soon beginning again.

And Griebel had to keep watch again, be on his guard, appeasing her, relenting, doing everything not to bring onto himself the "shame" that his wife had cracked up.

This complete abdication of his conviction was becoming hard for him. Sometimes an irrepressible agitation swelled in him, a fury. Then he blustered primly over annoyances at work, overburdening his people with work and anger. For he did not guess that this wrathfulness was no more than the anguish of his inner being, which was screaming for the peace which he had seen his father enjoy during his life.

A needless tension between the couple was increasing daily in severity, and in Griebel's forehead a vertical, sulky crease was digging itself deeper and deeper.

The pair struggled with each other like two invalids in mad, biting bitterness; like two sent out of their way, they talked in the meantime amicably and with sad sympathy to each other.

But everything furthered them just as irresistibly on the path to their unrelenting fate.

On the day after Ash Wednesday, which fell on 16 February, Griebel came home angrier than normal, threw his hat down on the commode and immediately began swearing and agitatedly striding back and forth in the room. Anna, who got in his way, was threatened with being thrown "straight out on the street with a bang". Griebel straightened up, jiggled his trousers lower with the energetic thighs of his short legs, spat, paused, shook his fist in the air with a terrible gesture and began roaming around the room again, constantly shifting the chairs and then thrusting them out of the way swearing.

"A beautiful arrangement!" he screamed at them seething.

"What's happening?" Leonore asked as she was entering and paused at the open door.

"Close the door!" Griebel growled dully, and when this had happened, he faced her firmly and screamed,

"And you? — Take care of the milk so that it doesn't sour. Understand ... if you want to anger me too!" he added gentler and began anew his wild foray of shoving chairs back and forth.

Leonore Griebel

With a feeling of distressing coldness, Leonore observed the unworthy outbreak of his agitation for a long time. Then she slowly asked, hard and constrained,

"At least tell me then what's happened?!"

Griebel continued his crashing around as though he did not hear a word from his wife in order to oblige her to repeat her question more urgently. But when this did not ensue, he paused, measured her with an astonished look and then began to tell her confusedly with a forced calm. At the same time, he was rushing back and forth. His wife had trouble understanding what it was about: a roll of thick woolen cloth had been accidentally cropped too close so that the coarse weave came through.

"I'll break all of the long-haired idiot's bones, or my name isn't Griebel!" he closed his telling. He was shaking both his fists, his face was white and his lips were trembling.

"Don't excite yourself so, you could take a blow!" Leonore admonished, now with greater sympathy.

"Yes — dammit! — excite myself — heavenly thunderbolts! — — No, you're right, Lorla, the boy isn't worth it. I'll leave quite tranquilly in the morning, open the door, step into the workshop, call the impudent lad over, look at the ass and say ... to, to him — thunders, I'll rip the animal's ears from his head!"

"But Joseph, is it worth making yourself sick over the boy?"

"Sickness comes, sickness goes! — I'm a man and won't allow myself to be played with, not by anyone. Understand?"

And he planted himself threateningly before her. After he had looked at her scathingly for a while, he began anew,

"Enough! I'll chase the rogue to the devil. He can rot in the street for all I care. I'll teach him to listen when I give an order."

Leonore could not help having an unpleasant feeling when she saw her husband trotting about in this fanatical rage, she was put in a huff by it and gazed steadily and grimly at him.

"Well yes!" he cried and turned suddenly to her brusquely so that she jumped. "Why are you looking so big-eyed at me? I won't devour him. He's too thin for that, hehe!" And he laughed for a long time, for his rage had suddenly changed into merriment.

There was then a knocking at the door.

"Was that a knock at the door?" he asked quickly and hushed.

"I think so,"Leonore answered bleakly, quickly putting the chairs in order, grasping her needle-work and alighting by the sewing table near the window.

The knocking repeated.

"Now, come in whoever!" the cloth maker called and cleared his throat.

"Hello, Mr Griebel! — You know me of course, Frank, from the firm Meyer and Sissel, Frankfurt on the Oder."

"Frankfurt? Frankfurt?" Griebel absorbed the words and lapsed into his old fury, "wonderful, but I'll take note and have a lot to say. Ha, you pulled a fast one with the indigo!"

"But, may I be permitted..."

"No you may not! What is that, permitted? I am the cloth maker Griebel, with me it's not permitted. In my house it's said simply: allowed. Understood? And I won't allow you to pull a fast one behind my back a second time!"

With that he began raging between the chairs again.

"But Joseph!"

Leonore threw him a reprimanding glance and rose. Her face was pale with shame. "Please, sit down!" she said to the stranger, "Don't take any offense, my husband has had some bother."

With a light gesture of her hand, she invited the disconcerted man to take a seat.

He bowed thankfully,

"Do I have the honour then of standing before Mrs Griebel? — Willy Frank, an old business friend of your good husband."

His lithe, lean body described the perfect lines of a gentlemanly bow. This reestablished his feeling of certainty, and with a winning smile, he laid the case of samples on the table, unbuttoned his overcoat and made himself comfortable on a chair whilst fondling his moustache.

Griebel, meanwhile, was walking back and forth between the chairs and self-consciously clearing his throat as though he was striving to overpower the eruption of his fury. The traveller sensed the peaceful urge of the accrued pauses and, half turned to the cloth maker, half to his wife, he began in a light, confident tone,

"Oh, I know, dear lady, your good husband doesn't mean it. I've known him far too long. He quite simply can't do without me."

"Oh you! — It just struck fifteen! — But no, it's just as if our man was an ape and didn't understand at all."

"But dear Joseph!"

"But now, I'd rather you said what loss you had with the indigo."

"Loss! — You probably think I want to reap something from it. That I don't need."

"God, but husband, you heard the man wants to make himself understood to you."

"Thank you, dear lady! — Of course I want that, Master! But let us put business aside for the time being. Come and tell me your bothers. Then everything will find itself."

He shoved a chair towards him and Griebel sat down in it because bringing this distressing scene to an end was obviously dear to him. For he had noticed how his wife's eyes had wandered a few times glowingly from him to the visitor, and he was frightened of there being an outbreak of "her nerves".

"Truly, what bothers can do!" Frank took the conversation up again, his voice having the ring of hearty concern. "But you look otherwise as fresh and young as a twenty year old."

"Now, now!" Griebel inserted in weak defense, flattered.

"Isn't that true, dear lady?"

Leonore just laughed softly, without looking up.

"With respect!" Frank cried quite strongly, taking her laugh as agreement. "Like a twenty year old! And I entered just now and was startled. Twenty years ago he looked older, really stupidly old. Take my advice, watch out by the way that you don't take a knock."

"You are right!" Griebel answered after a while, pressed and uncertain. "But what do you do then? That I'll tell you. After that you'll see yourself that it needs soaking in benzine."

And Griebel related the case in his long-winded way, weaving in the life history of the "cloth making bother", gave a detailed description of his workplace, came to speak for his choice of town councillor, in short, he galloped away. At the same time, he constantly had the feeling that

the traveller was making fun of him. In striving
to compel respect, his telling became more and
more confused, his gestures wilder and more
impassioned. But Frank bore the face of a devoted listener without being able to hinder a smile
from drawing gentle, mocking lines at the
corners of his mouth. In addition, he encouraged
him with interjections, "A madcap boy, that
one!" — "Simply awful!" — "I'm amazed at your
patience!" It was getting ever more distressing
for Leonore. She signalled furtively to her
husband to break off. It was no use. He talked
without break, and the listener was unconsciously brought into an ever merrier mood. What a
man! How he gently stretched his lithe limbs and
crossed his long, slender feet gracefully over each
other. How his white, delicate hand with its long
nails lead the cigar to his mouth. How his pointed, dark eyes looked through the little clouds of
smoke. That steep, white forehead in which a
lock of black hair hung! Through it the face, over
which a ringing acerbity lay, obtained a quiet
blessing. It offered an entirely innate charm to
her when he, as if listening seriously, let his
finely veined eyelids sink over his large, deep-
lying eyes. Then a restless tingling ran over the
delicate skin of his eyelids so that the long, black
lashes were constantly trembling. And that melo-
dious organ, a tenor, behind which the silence

shut itself with a lustful ripple ... in flight it saw, heard, felt everything.

"Isn't that right, dear lady?" Frank suddenly turned to her in order to invoke her participation in the conversation.

She flinched softly, lowered her gaze though immediately again and sat there shaking.

"Yes — yes — cer—tainly," she finally said and then pitched her dreamy eyes fervently at him.

"I have disturbed you in your labours. Please forgive me for that."

"Oh by no means!" she replied with stormily welling breaths. Finally she found the courage for her blindly erupting passion.

"I have seen you somewhere once before, long ago. You are as familiar to me as a brother, which you would have to be if I had one."

"Very flattering, very flattering!" Frank said, fetched out of his routine by this unexpected outburst.

"Now, watch it. Hey, my friend, don't you go enticing my wife away from me!" Griebel cried, forcing a laugh, and pulling the traveller heftily around by the sleeve.

The traveller had composed himself quickly and took up the interrupted conversation again,

"So completely depraved, Griebel, is that, is that not so?"

"Completely and utterly," he replied exhaling.

But Leonore looked steadily at the men with motionless, gleaming eyes.

Suddenly she began speaking dazedly, quietly, fumbling, numbed,

"Is it true you travel around the entire world?"

"What do you mean, dear lady?" the traveller turned around excited.

"Even by the deep, wide sea?" she continued in the happiness of a fervent fullness as though she had not heard his words, and she directed a large, deep, bright glance into his delicate face.

"Now it's coming over her!" The thought raced through Griebel's head. "Now quickly!"

"My wife, Mr Frank. Hey, listen to me! My wife is very interested, actually hugely, in such journeys, you must know. Especially the sea. — You must tell her everything another time. Now I must see to going to my workplace."

With these blatant words, the frightened cloth maker stamped down on the highly alarming moment and then gave his orders in rough haste.

"Now, however, I must be gone, and straight-away. Otherwise the bother will run off without having brushed the woolen cloth."

With that he stood up, and the traveller also rose visibly embarrassed while he grasped his things, musing. When he saw that Griebel was waiting most impatiently on his departure, he turned to Leonore in his most dashing pose,

"I give my regards to you, beautiful lady. I can tell you, from today on I believe in miracles. I saw you fleetingly once two years ago when you were still unmarried. On my honour, I did not recognise you. You have changed immensely to your advantage."

His eyes burned into her glowing face.

"May I be permitted to offer you my hand. Next time I will tell you with your permission about my travels. — You have a jewel, Griebel!" he called out, still holding Leonore's hand in his own, to the cloth maker who, completely stunned, was digging about in the clothes on the coat rack.

"Thunderbolts!" he grumbled as an answer, and since he had finally found his hat, he commanded, "But now out!" and trotted to the door.

With impassioned hesitance, Frank let go of Leonore's dazed hand and followed the hurriedly departed with deep bows toward the woman staying behind.

CHAPTER 11

Leonore Griebel

Between the molecules of air, a secret matter is hovering. It is receiving the heavy waves of human souls and reproducing them. It cannot be apprehended with any of the senses. We feel in it the excited soul-breathing of our neighbours. In quiet waves, it flows over us. Then we are able to know something whose understanding eludes us.

When Griebel returned home from his workplace, it was already dark and the town streets were livelier. For before the night comes, men become restive because a part of their life dies so quietly as the shadows of evening lengthen. To deaden their quite restrained fear, people tread noisier, speak louder and move their arms faster.

Griebel did not know why he walked so. When he exhaled, he paused, shook his head and then strode on slowly. At the door of his house, he hesitated, torn from a thoughtful slumbering, pulled his hand back hastily from the door handle and listened tensely to the hall. It was humming its old indistinct murmur. Sometimes a sharp bobbing leapt in-between. Then it twitched in Griebel, "Foolishness! ...", he said, finally pulling himself together unwillingly and stepping determinedly into the house.

It was dark. Even on the upper floor, the usual light was not burning. A feeling as though the walls were backing away when he touched them was becoming stronger and stronger. For that reason, he made for the bannister to get a hold on the light fixture. But although he made each step a bit more to the right as he rose, he did not reach the bannister. The steps seemed to have no end. Their height and depth also diminished from one to the other, so that he was stepping at first into emptiness only to find sure ground after a while.

Now it was going straight down — — and still no bannister ...

"Heavenly thunderbolts, light!" he finally cried in fury.

Far from him, a door flew open, a light tore its flickering eye upwards and immediately closed it in fright.

"Jesus, who ...?" screamed a female voice and broke off abruptly.

He was standing in the middle of the stairs and ... next to him a light sprang up from an endless walkway ... next to him ... out of the wall? ... he could hear his own breathing. — — He uncertainly took a long, groping step and — — bumped into a cold wall. He did not stir. A hot tingling, as though burning sand was flying into his face ... "sweet Hanna, the house witch!" ... it shuddered through his brain, although he bravely clenched his teeth.

"Dammit! Dammit! Dammit! In the name of God, the Father, the Son and the Holy Spirit. Amen!" he tried to ward off the ghost.

He drove the entire force of his feverish breath into this cry, and yet it sounded muted ... so the incantation was ineffectual.

The sand throwing became heavier.

Suddenly a red light flamed around him. An icy reflection came into his soul ... "what's going to happen now?" — The light was creeping up to him from his left, but he did not dare to turn around ... "now stop!"

... "now it's turning me around by the neck!" ... he thought in a cool self-composed way.

Then the scream of a female voice tore him from the clutches of mortal fear.

"Master, Joseph! Never such a thing! You're standing there and talking to the wall!"

It was the maid holding the light in her shaking hand. And he was standing at the opposite end of the hall in a corner.

"Joseph, you do not call me that ..." Griebel turned around instantly.

"Master, you're sweating! Yes, but everyone knows that this house is haunted."

"But when I tell you, it's *not* haunted?!"

"Well, then it isn't haunted, hahaha!" Anna laughed maliciously.

"Coarse hag!"

And Griebel stepped, breathing out, into the sitting room — —

The lamp stood with the flame wound down right on the edge of the table, by the sofa. A motionless, warm stuffiness met him as he entered the wearily lit room.

Leonore was still sitting at her place by the window, her hands in her lap with their palms laid on each other, her head bent forward as though searching for something. She did not seem to have moved in the five hours since his departure and did not stir either with his entrance.

"Good evening!" he said, "Dear!" he asked louder and straightaway added cautiously to himself, "you aren't listening!"

"... oh yes, lots — lots ..."

Hard of breath, she was speaking from a fast current in scattered surfacings.

"You, it's dark don't you know!" he growled and wound the lamp higher.

"... no, light ... light! ... light! ..."

In rising ecstasy, she talked to the floor and then slowly raised her head as though yielding to gentle pressure — — and — — started in fright.

"Yes, you're here already, dear Joseph! Well, good evening! Make yourself comfortable, I'll bring supper straightaway."

She then sprang up lightly. As though to violently shake off the spell of her intoxication, she took a few steps over to the table excitedly. Griebel sensed her erratically thrown attentions like the prattle of cool drips.

After the unpleasant scenes of the day, he was in an excitable state.

This gave way in an instant when he delved into the tasty supper which Leonore had placed invitingly on the fresh white tablecloth.

She did not eat with him and declared with the wonder of happiness in her voice,

"Oh God, how could I eat? — how could I? — how could I?"

Again and again she lovingly stroked the shimmering folds of the tablecloth down, tapped the vessels with nipping fingers, seized on Griebel's figure with a fervently groping glance and then, by an ever narrowing swing in her hips which looked like her body exulting, sank down into dreaming with her distracted upper body bent forward. Then she started,

"Couldn't flowers stand on the table? — Roses — carnations — perhaps violets — beautiful, simply beautiful — flowers — flowers!" —

"Yes, dear, flowers, in winter, and for what?" Griebel crudely answered the gentle words which Leonore had sung for him.

Then he shoved his plate away, and while he was letting with pleasure the belching of the savoured meal convulse his spongy body, he said jiggling, interrupted by many chirruping noises,

"Oh, that tasted good. — Well, I could take it up with him again. — But it was with Frank the traveller ... dear!"

"Yes!" Leonore leapt up, an unmoving glint in her large, pale blue eyes.

"... Dear ... dear ..." she repeated with expiring tenderness.

"Where were you looking then?"

"Well yes, simply ... it's simply ..."

Suddenly she was looking sharply at him, burning. Then she hesitantly stretched her arm out and touched Griebel's forehead with timid fingers as she stroked something away.

"What is it! Have I got something there? Anything is possible."

He walked to the mirror and observed his face.

"But everything is clear!" he said astonished. "Was something deceiving you?"

He turned around and fixed sharply on her.

She was sitting there with lowered head, and her bosom shivered in fearful waves.

With a disapproving air, he took a step back and then began walking back and forth on the runner between the commode and the bedroom door.

He was obviously pondering whether Leonore could endure the story of the ghost. In order to figure it out, he shook his trousers down a few times and snapped the fingers of his right hand behind his back.

The motionless, dull warmth of the high space was oppressing him so that he could not reach a decision.

Shyly, timidly, the big clock in the hall could be heard ticking. A high singing trembling followed each strike, and "n s s s", a delicate, contemplative tone then ran through the whole house.

"Something isn't right though in our house," he began hesitantly and looked over his shoulder at Leonore as he walked.

In silent agreement, she moved her lowered head back and forth.

"I was going up the steps," he finally began resolutely to recount, "up the steps," he repeated in a last qualm as his wife directed her eyes at him anxiously, "no, actually already at the door. I don't know now why I had to stop, I had to ..."

"When was that?" Leonore hastily interrupted him.

"Now, as I arrived."

"That's not right, he was already there," she said disappointed and leaned back in her chair.

"He? ... no. But listen first. — I was listening a little at the door. After that, stupidity, I thought, turn the handle and go in! The door flew open so that the hall seemed to bump. Then I paused for a moment. But there was nothing further. And I began to slowly go up the stairs, always close to the bannister. The light wasn't burning in the hall, and I thought, you can't fall from the way. — Well. — As I now grasped for the bannister, the wall started, it started and backed away ... why did you screw the light down, Lorla?"

"The better to listen."

She says it in impatient haste, and her gaze adheres stickily to his lips.

"... the wall started and backed," she urges him on from where he paused.

Griebel perceives her excitement in dismay, and because he believes he would make the calamity still worse by suddenly breaking off, he continues uncertainly,

"Actually no, it was just as though the wall ..."

Now Leonore springs to her feet with signs of fervent approval, and to the cloth maker it is as though a hotly intruding wave is forcing the timid words back into his mouth.

Overwhelmed, he breaks off.

Her hands entwined, her head inclined devotedly, the woman is standing there.

But no human sound stirs her.

The ticking is timidly reminding, the long, fine tone begins piningly like the echo of a song dying away in ever weaker waves.

Then she raises her head pregnantly. Her hand is caressing her hair from her opposite temple. Upright, with head bent back, she remains for a while.

With the pining song of that fine tone she then continues, "... a wind rose in me and picked up all the walls in which my soul was sick, all the shadows in which it almost died ... like it was flowering at once and sounding ... the light rose and fell like white virgins between the trees, they fondled it with their leaves ... but after that it came ... the forest closed ranks, the earth stretch- ed out and it all became *him*. Only the light stayed around him ... just like he sat there in front of you today, next to me, with the black lock on his ..."

Suddenly her overrunning speech broke off. She was staring rigidly at the wall. Then she raised her hands pointing and whispered with shivering lust,

"He is returning here ... here — here — ah! — Yes — just wait! ... come! — — — you ... too! Just go there, I'm coming ..."

Her arms outspread encompassingly, with falling steps, her lips moving silently, her face transfigured, she disappears into the bedroom.

With trembling hand, Griebel bolts the door behind her, then he also closes the door to the hall. Now he is standing in the sitting room again, listening. Nothing stirs inside. — — "She is pitching herself through the window!"

In quietest haste, he opens the door again.

Leonore is standing motionless in front of her bed.

"This will be the last time ... oh never! ... Griebel, Griebel; I shouldn't think the worst."

Now, is she talking again? — Yes! —

A furtively tender whispering.

Suddenly a chasm opens in him. From it the smouldering flame of a terrible idea closes in on him. After the birth, when she was lying in bed, had she not then said something like, as though he did not need to be ... and her incomprehensible behaviour of the past months would all simply be ... and now! — now ... in confused scraps, certainly and torturing, it was boiling down in him. In order not to notice, he throws his entire strength into listening. And as he stands and listens, he consoles himself again, "It was probably just her nerves. They tend to be just so. My God, such a collected girl as she was ..."

But he broke off sharply, for she was now starting to talk out loud.

At first he did not understand anything, just stammering noises — — but now! — —: "Oh—h!

— — Dear ... dear ...! you too? ... do you see! ... perhaps even as a little girl ... I know, how long ago, then you were already mine."

Now there was was nothing left to guess!

He rushed up to her and seized her arm,

"Stop!" he roared, "stop!"

Leonore jumped in fright and looked at him anxiously.

"Who are you talking to? — Confess! confess! — — Perhaps with that man Frank?" he continued after a silent hesitation.

"Shouldn't I?" his wife asked gravely with surprise.

"So then!" he now shouted, rushing without pause. "Shouldn't you? — Yes, you don't want to know that such a thing is adultery? — Hey? — — Some people do that, but not my wife."

In his rampant fury, he did not notice how Leonore was shivering under his grasp.

"Adultery, do you understand! — In my house, that doesn't happen!"

"Am I committing adultery?" Leonore finally asked with icy voice through gritted teeth and shoved his hand from her arm.

"Yes, such thoughts are adultery, a mortal sin."

"Oh yes — in your soul, is that true? — Truly?"

Her face had shrunk. In chaste fear, she was asking her husband with trembling lips.

"Adultery," the cloth maker repeated dully.

"No. Something that is so beautiful can't be bad. I don't believe it!" she pondered and shook her head.

After a long, long pause, she raised her tear-filled eyes,

"But, trust in your wife — — go to bed in peace, go!"

Shocked, he grasped the right hand she offered. She sank into the chair and lapsed into a rigid gaze.

Griebel began to potter about helplessly, dismayed, in sorrow, full of remorse and shame. In vain he tried to talk himself into believing he had behaved correctly. To escape this torturous state, he extinguished the light and lay down in bed. But his wife did not stir.

He listened tensely for a long time to her every breath.

Hours later she rose ... "no, not! — but it will be difficult for me!" he heard her say to herself. Then he heard her getting undressed.

CHAPTER 12

Leonore Griebel

That night Griebel slept as though on the threshold of an open front door, troubled by being half awake and dreaming at the same time.

He was often startled abruptly from a short sleep when a noise sounded so fine and agonising that he opened his eyes in fright. But then he heard only the calm breaths of the large sleeping house around him which were blowing away out into the street. In the end he was lying there with large, dry eyes until he became aware of two grey spots in the night, which he did not know if he dreamt or saw. To calm himself down, he decided to take them for windows. Only they were transforming themselves into the open calyxes of autumn crocuses. After they had been blooming quietly for a while, their black stems began to move, swaying. In order not to be hurled from the flower in which he sat, he crept down a stem as a big, green grasshopper. He had transformed himself intentionally into this insect because he found a better hold on the delicate smoothness of this plant with the sharp claws of his feet. It also pleased him to create an aching tremor in it because every step was a wounding. But when he had reached the base of the sharp leaves, he was annoyed about his naked, club-like thighs. The flowers laughed at him mockingly over them. It sounded so completely clear that, waking, he listened for the echo in the quiet room.

Only there was nothing.

Then he felt as though someone was listening to him. The large, avid eyes of discomfort were sucking on his brain. Everything rising in him was swept away by it as though by a wind. The last to dance out was a church tower which a hound was running after howling. It was whining like a man.

Agonised, Griebel got up.

Then the sound died away with a noise into the corner. — "Lorla, is it you?" he asked, but fell silent straightaway, as his voice seemed strange to him, like the noise of clumsy hands drumming on a wooden cask.

Finally the terrible night was gone and the grey of the germinating morning soothed him.

But hardly had his consciousness settled into this calm than the play began anew. The veil of the dawn transformed into a dancing whirlwind which heaped up with invisible arms white, wafting garments from the loose snow over which it surgingly drove.

The cloth maker knew quite well that its noise did not come from the wind, but rather stemmed from a bed which someone was hesitantly rumpling. But in a state which was as much fervid curiosity as exhaustion, he remained quite still and let the whirlwind constantly dance past him.

Now it did not sound at all like a whirlwind anymore. It was speaking swallowed words from the heavy breaths of adversity, then it knelt down by his bed and sank into a painful silence.

Its blond hair lay on its two bare, sweet arms which still shook from the echo of the dance; even its head was trembling from it. And a shimmering tremor was gliding thus through its long, golden hair, over the white dress and storing itself in the shaking of its soft folds into infinity. Now it was raising its head so that its face could be seen: its large, frozen eyes were full of tears falling now and then on his bed covers ... "Jesus Maria! wasn't that his wife?" ...

Only now it was standing up, quite, quite gently, like only whirlwinds can, and stretching, stretching up to the heavens, always looking at him with a deep, fixed gaze from its frozen blue eyes. Then it stretched its hands out and stroked his hair so that he lost his senses in horror ... "heaven is with you and with me — — with me — oh! with me — — with ...", as it said that with its deepest throes, it was seized by an ever faster circling dance and disappeared with a loud bang.

Griebel actually awoke with that and sat up in bed.

Had it been a dream or had Leonore been standing before his bed?

Yes, she was already up. She was just calling for the maid, "Anna! — get up!" — So it could have been her; but where was the need for her to pray over him as though a great misfortune lay over them both?! — Suddenly the events of the previous day occurred to him. They occurred to him like a wild dream. But it did not help; he really had seized her by the arm and shaken her in extreme rage because she had rambled on about that traveller in such suspicious ways. Perhaps it had been quite stupid of him, and yet he gave himself the right, but always so, as if actual relations existed between his wife and this man, for which he had not the slightest evidence.

In any case, he must see how his wife conceived the whole affair. He promptly left his bed and got dressed.

In the kitchen he learnt that she was just then going to matins and would be returning somewhat late. He would just have to breakfast in peace alone.

Leonore Griebel

He did not succeed in having a discussion with Leonore. He heard her elusively going and giving her orders quietly in the nursery. He waited for her behind the corner of the passages into the hall. Only the success of his best plans was frustrated by an unexpected occurrence or by Leonore's attentiveness, which knew every time to arrange the thrusting of a third person between her husband and herself. She did not seek her bed until after his falling asleep and distanced herself before he awoke, or stayed all night with the boy when he had once timidly made the attempt to negotiate with her over the matter.

Then her haste was a little more urgent and trembling; her words less sure; her gaze shyer.

But everything lay in the bonds of an ever sweet smile, a smile which sometimes sobbed shaking because the strain which stretched and and eased its light-shifting waving lines was being felt too much.

Was the pulling together of everything the confirmation of her guilty conscience or her unforgiving animosity? In the fever of conflicting emotions, Griebel only kept with effort the mask of his clumsily dignified good nature.

He walked around as though with a hot morsel in his throat which was torturing him infinitely and yet which he must not spit out. For the first time in his life, a burden was oppressing him which did not yield to the handling of his inherited principles.

Before the fact of disloyalty, vanity, dread, shame and fear closed his eyes for grief and worry. And he denied it with the loud and trite reasons of his conscience. But he could not stop his soul from creeping furtively in hard breathing unrest to the abyss from which the feverish haze of blind misgivings climbed which fed on him greedily.

Every day the weight of his secret increased. An empty urge to move which looked like work zeal drove him from half-finished thing to half-finished thing, badgered the dignity of his short-legged stride into fitful hacking steps, took the ease of digestion from his stomach and tingled the slack fat of his long cheeks with an unbearable twitch.

Finally he was worn down to the point of owning up to and regretting every wrong as committed. In this mood, old Mrs Marsel still had to ask him,

"Won't Lorie see me at all?"

"Well yes — oh — she — I don't know, she isn't herself anymore for working so hard."

"How did that happen? — And every day that God gives, she goes to matins. She just flies past."

Yes, yes! — His circumstances tortured him to burning. He must at least suggest something to relieve himself. So he started after a pause of looking bleakly,

"Look at me!" With that he pulled the lower edge of his vest from his sloping belly. "Well! I have dwindled so. Already more of a ribbon than a man."

In deepest spiritual hardship, his lips were trembling.

"Jesus!" the old woman cried, seized him by the arm and attempted to pull him into the shop.

But Griebel suddenly recognised the error he had committed,

"Oh, don't be frightened! Everything is okay. No, no. But so much work, so much work, bothers with workers and — I haven't been well in a long time. But don't worry yourself over it. Sometimes just having such a small cough seems healthy. — Adieu, I have to go to my work."

He broke off brusquely, gave her his hand and disappeared hurriedly behind the next corner.

***

Now her mother had become suspicious and was following Leonore.

She threw to her the hook of a shout on the street and appeared at all hours under an inane pretext to ask after her. She pinged the small shop bell quickly again at the door, but excuses throve poorly in her tortured soul and her trembling heart only for a short time found the courage to dismiss pity.

With every spiritual hardship, Leonore had relaxed in the thought of her mother.

"... I will throw myself on her breast, will tell her everything, and she will console me ..."

So the tormented woman had thought in the moments of greatest distress.

Now she recognised in her maternal worries that her certainty had only been the wish of her helpless need.

My God, it is all dissolving into shadows.

The confessor had proffered her an oath over her love for Frank. And she vowed it a thousand times praying in the convulsions of her heart, but the poison of all the imprecations which she painfully forced out were etching the image of the black haired one even more luminously. Alone she battled in faith until faint.

With staggering steps, the glimmer of the ascetic in her watchful eyes, Leonore then crept to the cradle of her boy and bent her knees before it. In the whirl of a turbid despair, she twined her hands over the sleeping child and stuttered futilely, "Never, my dear Gustav, never! No, your mother won't do it! He would not simply have come, he — he, oh God, if I could just swear, he!"

And his image swims into her on the clouds of her torment, and all her senses trail with the ardency of thirst over it.

She rises with racing pulse, glowing cheeks. She amasses all the power of her trembling soul and hurls barren imprecations at him ... but her oath turns into stammers of desire; her knees slacken from their defiant step, and the prayer of her earthward wrestled hands swings up into jubilation.

Her renouncing gives birth to her forbidden love, and her oath makes her desire for loyalty powerless.

"My God, Mrs Griebel, why have you been whimpering this fortnight when you're alone? the nurse asked.

"Headaches, Kathrine, nothing but headaches."

"Yes, how do we get headaches? You're not catching a cold, you know yourself ... how is your stomach?"

"Oh no ..., but you don't know sometimes if it really is a headache. It can also seem to be something else entirely."

"No, Mrs Griebel, from head to toe — the torso — the heart — — now, the heart — I would think that'd be possible."

Leonore laughed lightly like a string stretched to breaking wails when a fat finger strikes it, and then she discreetly took flight. —

Oh, and in her most secret moments she hatched in the play of her imagination a plan which she conceived in the warping of her pain with the pure, strong breath of deliverance: — — — — — — — — — — — — — the supervision of the first morning hours had led her to her bed again after nights of being waylaid and wandering about. The entire sweetness of her forbidden desire had become a burdensome pressure on her temples. —

The night wind was reeling through the streets, a homeless vagabond who drunkenly screams the turbid sensation of its misery, with ever open mouth, in dissipated tones, lulled senseless. Then it thunders at the doors and desires entrance with whirling fists. And it always begins again its restless round with the helpless whining from between frost-shattered teeth.

The Griebel's house threatens it in vain with the cold vehemence of its lightning rods; futilely drives the whirring from its protective covers.

Again and again the hearthless one pushes against the great doors so that their round window eyes shimmer a grim green in the light of the tired old moon. Old time cannot sleep at all and, in the short moments of silence, shuffles its dragging steps across the soundless hall.

Then Leonore feels pinched, and her breath comes roughly like from under a heavy stone.

She had begun several times already to put away her clothes, but stopped again startled when the old clock outside counted the hour alone with hoarse voice.

And when she is finally finished undressing, the thought suddenly comes to her that it is quite absurd to do so. With a weak smile, she wipes away the oddness of this thought and squirms under the covers.

She waits dully for sleep. Meanwhile the dislodged reproach assumed its true face and returns to her again. Now she recognises it. "Truly, I would have gone to sleep."

Soft as thread, she is already out of bed, across the blankets with fumbling arm, out into the sitting room to the chair by the window. Like three weeks before, her wide eyes look at the table opposite her which peers out of the night with the gentlest of outlines. But what succeeded a hundred times, fails today. She does not see him anymore as he sits there and caresses the dark locks from his beautiful, high forehead with his white, slender hand.

Under the pounding of the night storm his image, which wanted to climb germinating out of the darkness with uncertain lines, flies away.

After that she listens to the long sound of the space traveller wandering away again into the streets which are scrunching its deep moans into inarticulateness with the heavy jaws of stony row houses.

"Go away ... away!!" —

Her too?

A pleasant shock, like the bliss of a redemptive lightning bolt falling from a heavy cloud. —

"Away ... away! ... away!!" — The storm entices with the loud wounds of its freedom, and the narrowness around her closes in on her with the mumbling of dull, indolent warmth, the fat snoring sounds of her husband, the bleakness of the charmless space, the quite dreary utility of her being, this marriage without fragrance, this lazy affluence, these eyeless days lacking sun ... "away" ... she slips into her dress, goes and packs a bundle of necessities, kisses the wall to the nursery in which the nurse rocks the cradle humming, and hurries to the stairs. But she pulls her gliding body back from the second step and seeks out the bedroom. — No, she must take leave of her husband. Who knows, he loves her still; only he has no gift for expressing his love.

He lies on his left side, his face towards the room. His blond moustache bristles with rustling exhaled breaths, and his right arm rests on the covers.

"Heaven give you forgetfulness! — God bless you!" she thinks with searching eyes. At the same time, she strokes his hair quite gently. With that Griebel groans long and heavy, his dream-lamed lips murmur incomprehensibly, and then the dreary song of his sleep begins again.

Leonore escapes quietly through the door, clasps the bundle tighter outside, purses her lips and boldly takes up her flight again.

She moved in poor, poor she will go. Only her life is rescuing her, her honour, his honour, the good name of her mother. Just then she begins to turn the rusty key. It is completely silent and the shrill grating with which the key turns in the lock makes a racket up the stairs. For that reason, she does not dare to continue and waits on a new blast of wind; then she unlocks it fully. But just then, when she wants to slip onto the street, heavy steps sound from its other end.

Two figures — deep, swollen, male voices — in muffled play of question and answer. They come nearer. One is the night watchman, the other is unknown. She looks out through a small crack in the door.

It is quite calm.

"... hey!"

"Yes, yes, — in a ditch. For pity, you could hear it from a distance."

"Oh, never!"

"What I said! — There's nothing to 'oh, never!' When I say for pity, it's true."

"Well, and how does it go on?"

"Like this ... listen up! Is that the cloth maker Griebel's house?"

"Indeed it is."

"Listen now how his child flares up, high, sore, as though his mother was dying that moment ..."

"You, have you ever seen her now?"

"No! Stop, I have to tell you the rest of it. The child in the ditch was from ..."

The conversation became incomprehensible ... Leonore turned closely and slowly into the street and looked rigidly at the men stumbling away.

Her deliverance was a crime — — —

Cautiously and steadily, she closes the front door again from within. With humbly obedient head, her arms slack, lacklustre steps, she hauls herself back to her cell, unfolds her bundle and hangs her dress up in its place.

A cold numbness, an inexplicably bitter impotence shakes her like a feverish chill.

She cannot warm herself in bed.

Dull despair lies on her and she ponders the ground before her stupidly like a prisoner who hears the straw of his misery rustling under him after an unsuccessful escape attempt.

Thus thrown back by a power which was from her and yet not of her, the torturous feeling of complete abysmalness came over Leonore more and more forcefully and pushed her more and more towards her mother, towards her family.

But it was also a trait of a weak conscience which was taking possession of her like an intrusive dissonance cleaving the fullness of a jubilant orchestra.

Oh, what did she know anyway?

Her will rushed her about according to the emotions which rose sometimes from this, sometimes from that corner of the morals she had been taught.

After such wilted days, she threw herself exhausted and seeking help again and again from her great passion into the arms which rushed through her depths.

And — her husband crept cowardly and idly around her struggle. A fond, cheerily bestowed word could have strengthened her and led her back. At least she thought so. Or, if he could only have brought himself to a reckless blow!

Nothing but this cautious creeping, this quiet insect-like scurrying in her shadow.

Everything in her had rebelled, but everything was deserting her.

*****

"Oh mother!"

With this cry, which she spoke softly because her heart was crying so, she threw herself in her mother's arms. She had walked unwittingly out of her husband's house and was now clasping the withered body of her mother with morbidly hard tension. — It quivered under her. When Leonore felt that, she pulled her coursing sorrow back into her raw breast, pushed away the body of this adorable person as far as her arms permitted, and looked her in the eye, quite deeply.

"I am very, very happy, mother!"

"Is that why you don't come over to me anymore? — True, isn't it?"

"Mother — oh, I — am — happy — happy — Jesus Maria!"

She stiffened and her voice turned shrill.

After a dead moment, she turned away and left the shaken woman alone.

But in the old room, she then strode up and down for hours.

"What have I done! — What have I done!" And she wrung her hands.

CHAPTER 13

Leonore Griebel

Griebel resided inertly, undisturbed in the certainty of his intention to "settle" with Leonore at a favourable moment.

The entire affair began to peter out for him. Why should he also "stir it up unnecessarily" when nothing pointed to a scandal.

He had already been alone at the table a few times with his wife. She was looking pale, but not tired. No, there was a sharpness to her entire being. And if he wanted to pass from the tepid circles of their faltering conversation to private matters, he always had to fall silent though.

Her unusually gleaming eyes, whose blue seemed to have become much deeper, hindered him from doing so. Then he drew back his index finger which had been fumbling around the edge of the plate,

"Let's leave it a little still."

But always, when her anxiously flaming look had so nullified his inert courage, his leisureliness turned into embarrassment.

He saw how she grew weary afterwards, as though a last, weak hope had deceived her. She sat there and stared at her lap, tore herself away violently and looked somewhere else. And in the midst of her bewilderment, she emitted words like, "Take a few more berries!" The cry began stifled and ended with a tormented laugh so that the fat man was seized by an impregnable fear of his wife, who then abruptly sprang up and rushed to her bedroom.

One evening Griebel was returning later than normal from his work.

The waning day was lying in broad, dissolving shadows next to the calmer houses and it began to fall asleep. Windless snow fell thickly through dully chilled deep twilight. The inflated traffic of the small city took on a touch of loud merriment. You stretched your hand out and let the biting snow melt away on your warm skin. But then it is quite pretty when it snows so quietly in March again. Only those looking at the sky made a grumpy face.

"What do *you* think, Mr Griebel! I think I don't believe the fine snow. Look out, before the hand turns it'll turn unpleasant," a local smith addressed the earnestly pacing cloth maker after both men had shaken hands.

"Oh, from where, smith."

"Now, you look out, Griebel, if tomorrow there isn't weather in which a dog would die outside, then call me Ignaz."

"And if there is, I will. If only it could turn into spring."

"Yes, when it will ..."

"Oh well, when it will. As you say, smith! There hasn't been a year without a spring at all."

"Yes, it's always on the calendar. But, but ... for example, what was it like in '63?"

And, as they walked, the smith began to tell the story of a year without a spring, "All the blossoms were brown on the trees. The leaves hung black on the branches. The birds were falling out of the sky. The grain had no ears for all the snow and cold. My father sowed eight sacks full, and he could only raise four. You could count it on your fingers. We lived at the time in Scharfeneck."

They had then arrived in the vicinity of the Griebel house.

The cloth maker saw his mother-in-law pacing back and forth before the house with every sign of anxious impatience.

"Yes, yes — it can happen like that," Griebel replied distracted.

"Well, we part here then. Good night!"

And he headed humbly for old Mrs Marsel.

When she recognised him, she stepped hastily through the open door into the house.

The cloth maker followed her just as silently with that tremor in the region of his stomach which always beset him in critical moments and which was marked by a pounding heart. He closed the door and after a step stood silently in the darkness.

"Well?" he asked roughly in the direction from which suppressed sounds of fear were ringing out.

"What's happened, mother?" he repeated with his breath tailing off after a hesitant pause in which he received no answer.

"Holy, blessed mother! — Oh God no! — Don't hold it against me! I can't help it. I can't! I did everything. Joseph —"

And while the desperate woman was stuttering it breathlessly, her hand sought for his.

Now her trembling, cold right hand was clutching his limply sagging hand.

Their souls' lives were becoming entwined.

"When did she jump out then?" Griebel asked mutely.

"Oh Jesus no ..."

And as if his question had been affirmed, he continued quietly in blind desolation,

"Is she quite dead?"

He was asking this under the burden of a fate whose fulfillment he had held onto with the intractable superstition of a constricted nature.

But the simple, terrible "yes" did not come. On the contrary, the truth wrestled itself lisping from the tormented mother's lips,

"I was just carrying the finished bread into the shop. My assistant had fallen asleep. It was about two, you had left barely half an hour before, when Anna plunged into the shop and cried, 'Marsel mother,' she cried, 'but quick, something's happened with the lady.'

The bread fell from my hands with the shock. Before I could ask, the maid was already outside again and hurrying across the street.

As I came in, I didn't know my soul anymore. I was almost on hands and knees coming up the stairs. And there both maids were standing in the hall by the clock case and wringing their hands.

'But for what does she need money if she wants to do something to herself?' the nurse asked me. 'I had to lend her twenty marks.'

I thought, the woman wants to kick out from her unhappiness, don't look first, go to the door and listen. At first it was dead still. But then when after a while I knocked and called, she began and acted as if she was dying. I asked, I threatened, I cried. What a mother wouldn't do for her child out of fear!

But when I heard that she had little Gustav still in with her, I was overcome, wedged my fingers in the crack of the door so that they bled, pushed, scratched the wood with my nails, I ..."

Then Griebel seized her by the arm,

"My dear little son too?"

She fell silent before the torment of this cry.

In the street, a troop of children ran past laughing. Suddenly a young voice began screaming. "Lift him up, Bertha!" an older boy ordered reluctantly.

After that only the blurred sounds of the small city traffic could be heard again.

"... my dearest little son!"

With the ardency of his paternal love, Griebel fortified the senses of his numbed courage.

Then he said decisively, "Come!" and drew her towards the stairs.

At the first step, she abruptly broke free and stopped in the uncertain light of the little hall lamp whose glow was melting away pitifully into the night.

"Hey, Joseph, why has it all come to this?"

"Why — yes, why ... why ..."

He shook his head at the ground,

"That I can't say myself."

Mrs Marsel did not ask anything more, and they entered the hall.

Griebel was making heavy strides, like someone in distress creating a firm sound in order to keep his senses clear.

"Go to the maids in the kitchen so that they don't come out and carry every detail around the entire city. — I will see if she will let me in," he whispered, and, spurred on inwardly, he added quietly, "It must come to an end."

The old woman pressed his hand silently and disappeared into the kitchen.

He paused for a moment at the door to the sitting room. He coughed a few times irresolutely. Finally he drew strength, tucked his trousers in his boots, stamped a few times energetically and then bent down to the door handle ... "Lor — hm ... Lorie! ... dear! ..." he said quite mildly so that his held breath pressed against his soul. He straightened up and let it out carefully.

Then it seemed to him as though something was stirring inside.

She still lives! —

In joyful haste, he knocked with his crooked index finger and called as loud as his caution would permit, "Now open up!"

A hesitant groan answered from within.

"Open up, what must the maids be thinking!"

He heard someone in the kitchen, speaking loudly, going to the door.

"... yes, albeit, you should have seen though how wild ..."

It was Anna's screechingly hard voice.

Any moment the curiosity of one of the girls could be dislodged, despite the vigilance of the mother, and then he would be found standing in front of the door like a hound.

"Thunder ..., damm..., thunderbolts..., Lorla! I'll force the door open if you don't open up straightaway!" he puffed agitatedly through the crack in the door and pressed himself against it so that the panel on which his shoulder pressed creaked, as those steps like before approached the kitchen door.

Otherwise it was completely silent. Only something like a quietly seething hissing was passing through the garrets.

Then that fell silent too.

Finally a shuffling step from within came towards the door and stopped before it.

The clock was about to strike the hour.

"When the clock strikes, she'll have a think and won't open up," this strange thought seized him forcefully so that he noiselessly sprang to it and stopped the pendulum.

Then he reached for the little hall lamp on the bread cabinet.

Now the bolt was quietly drawing back.

"If the child still lives," he stuttered quietly to himself. With pounding heart, slowly so that the naked little flame did not perish in the act, he entered and immediately shut the door again behind himself.

He bumped his knee on a chair with his first steps so that the little lamp flickered and threatened to go out.

"I don't want to break my neck," he said hastily because he did not know what else to say.

"Where are you then, hey? You could at least say 'good evening'!"

He took a step forwards and again bumped against a chair which he only saved from tipping over by quickly grasping its backrest.

Still he did not see his wife. The smouldering flame of the little lamp, which he was holding up by the right side of his face, was dazzling his searching eyes which were not able to distinguish anything outside an absurd circle of light. That's why he placed it carefully on the table. Now the light steadied and its red bloom flowed out to the walls of the room.

Now he was distinguishing everything exactly. Everything was in disarray from the struggle. The chairs were standing about as though they had run in despair awkwardly into each other with their stiff legs. The table cloth was hanging crookedly so that a corner touched the floor. Silver coins lay strewn across its top. A few had fallen to the ground as though they had been thrown in disgust. At the other end of the table, the small needle case sat, and the ring with its red stone lay next to it.

Items of clothing were hanging over all the chair backs, a mess from being hung up and taken back. The sofa cover was crumpled into confused rolls, the curtains had been partly torn from the rods by knotted fingers.

Leonore was leaning stiffly against the wall next to the cupboard. As if she knew that Griebel, once he had scanned everything, would direct his gaze at her, she caught it with large, motionless eyes. An unspeakably painful smile filled her face at the same time.

"Jesus Maria, Lorla!"

Suddenly the cramp eased which had leaned her against the wall. A slackness transformed the stiff dry expression on her face, and Griebel watched as she sank down. She wrestled herself arduously back up, but could not hold herself up anymore.

Griebel quickly pushed a chair over to her and she fell in it, tired and heavy. Her head bowed forward and her pale hands propped themselves on her trembling knees.

He stood silently for a while next to her.

"Where is little Gustav?" he then asked unnaturally dulled.

At first she nodded staring at the ground, and when she raised her face to him, it still carried those rigid features.

"I thought so." She said it quietly, but with a shaking bitterness. "Go, father — mph! — go, he's lying in my bed!"

When she then saw him kissing the boy again and again in overflowing joy, the last tears still remaining to her crept slowly, seething down into the bleached folds of her unspeakably painful smile.

"Lorla! — Lorla!" Griebel called with vibrating larynx and showed her the cradled child as if he had to bring to her attention this unexpected discovery whose preciousness she had no idea of.

"I have to show the boy to mother!" and he sought his way past her to the door.

"*Where* are you going?"

Bolt upright, resolute, threatening, she stood in his way.

"Mother? My mother?" she asked again and looked firmly at him.

"Well, why not then?"

"If it isn't enough, she should still ..."

Then she lapsed into thought.

"Good," she started resolutely, "go and tell my mother, Lorie gives her her kindest regards."

With that she stepped to the side and began resolutely to dress.

Meanwhile the kitchen door opened and the voice of old Mrs Marsel could be heard.

Leonore started, tore the half donned jacket off again and hurriedly cleared everything in the bedroom up again.

Griebel understood.

"Yes, yes, your mother mustn't know," he said and help her put the room in order.

After that, when Mrs Marsel entered cautiously, only a little of the previous state was could be observed. Only the ring still lay on the table and a few silver coins had been forgotten on the floor.

In leaving the bedroom, Griebel pushed the portière to the side with his right hand and watched as Leonore, having just finished lighting the table lamp, turned affectionately to her mother.

"It's so nice of you to come, mother. Good evening!"

And she kissed her on the forehead with a passion which looked so hot because her movements had lost nothing of their hardness and were struggling arduously out of a stony constraint. "Come, sit down!" she continued talking unusually loud and compelled her mother into a chair while she took her place on the other side of the table. In sitting down, she pushed the lamp away from herself so that the faces of both women were in the light shadow of the pink lampshade.

After that she began to speak,

"Yes, it was a terrible — terrible — oh — headache. — I — ah — heard you knocking, you and the maids. — But — ah — oh God, what do you know? ... right! — You howled too as if I were already dead — dead ... dead! — Look ... why? ... it isn't gone yet ... it makes one quite confused. — — —

Why did I borrow the money from the nurse? — Twenty marks ... as if I had wanted to make a journey ... isn't it, Joseph! — But for my dear husband ... husband!! — I would not have opened up. All the clothes still lay over the chairs ... The money is still lying there ...”

She said it shaking. It was meant to sound innocently trifling. She looked at her fingers and scratched with the nails. From time to time, when she thought herself unobserved, her eyes stole weakening to her mother. With that her talk became more and more quavery.

A pause followed, during which Griebel and Mrs Marsel exchanged worried looks, Leonore though looked at her hands, the tips of whose index fingers she was pressing tightly together.

As though spurred, she tore her head up,

“My dear, dear mother!” and mused sadly over the sound of her voice which died away weak and pleading.

“No, I said it like that as a child — — yes! as a — child ... as a child, it was a different then too.”

“Oh yes,” Mrs Marsel finally engaged in the conversation, “different, better, better, yes hm ... hm ...” but she broke off because she knew where it was going.

After a short think, she shook off the clever evasiveness and set off in her old crudeness straight to the point.

"Hey, what's this all about? What must people think? Aren't you good to your husband?"

Thus her worry broke forth stonily. At the same time, she looked bellicosely at Leonore.

"Good?" Leonore asked, sprang up, flung her arms around her unsuspecting husband's neck and kissed him tempestuously. She pressed her body feverishly against his and stammered sweet nothings.

"Mother, she's biting me! — Lorla, it hurts!" Griebel cried for help.

"But girl!" Mrs Marsel seized her hard by the shoulder and tore her away. "Truly, my soul, I can see teethmarks on his cheek. There and there, —" and she felt her son-in-law's face which sat there quietly and looked up at her resignedly as if he wanted to say, 'now see, she's always doing it'.

But the old terror had come over Leonore heavier after this morbid outbreak of tenderness, and she stood impassively to the side, her hands folded tensely as though she was keeping to herself, her gaze directed at the floor.

"Now could someone do that who has no love in their heart?"

She said it mutely and looked fixedly from one to the other.

With that she dropped down into her seat and said, "My mother ..." again so weakly, trembling like a child afraid of ghosts calling for help.

Only her mother misunderstood her.

"I believe it, Lorie. But not too hot and not too cold, pretty wise. — See, you've already been married three years. I think it must've already occurred to you. You are still healthy."

The boy in the bedroom had awoken and was crying. At this sound, Leonore started. Then she looked tensely at her husband.

He sprang up hastily at the same time as the old woman and their cries rang out simultaneously,

"Jesus, little Gustav!"

"Well now, my little son!"

"Oh God!" nobody saw how Leonore pressed her entwined hands against her bosom in bitter disappointment.

Then she abruptly stood up and took a few shuffling steps towards the bedroom from which her mother was coming with the boy on her arm and the beaming cloth maker alongside. — Now the little boy had to do all the tricks which the nurse had taught him: display moods, where his little heart was, the skyfather, how big he is ...

Griebel and her mother were quite boisterous, laughing too loud, clapping their hands, and the fat man even leapt up awkwardly once to make Gustav laugh.

But it was all the overloud, pricking cheerfulness of hidden sorrows.

Leonore was following the scenes with a forced smile.

Several times she tore the little boy hastily out of her husband's arms and handed him to Mrs Marsel.

"You're jealous, perhaps" Griebel finally asked in jest.

"Ass!!"

It tumbled like a curse from Leonore's lips.

"But Lorie, did your mother teach you that?"

"Oh you, why does he talk so stupidly!"

Finally she could not bear the caresses her child was experiencing anymore.

Shrilly she called for the nurse and, when her disconcerted face appeared in the open door, declared that the boy must now have his meal as he is accustomed. She, his mother, must know that. Then they could do with him what they wanted.

And when the three then, just as embarrassed as to begin with, again sat peacefully at the table, Leonore began anew when she saw how her husband was getting ready to speak.

He obviously wanted to say something jovial, as he smacked his full lips cheerily slurping.

Then Leonore interrupted him hastily,

"How did the story of the knight go, mother, the one you told me when I was still a child?"

"Which then?" the old woman asked, unsure.

"Now listen! Was it like this: A knight had a wife and a child. He was fond of both and was poor. It was a long time ago, and he served the emperor with body and soul. Then a great war came, and the emperor said to the knight, 'Come and help me. You have a wife and child, and if you come to me and go along with me to the war then you could die and your wife and child will perish. But, will you go with me all the same?'

Then the knight knelt down, kissed the emperor's hand and said merely, 'My emperor!' After that he stood up, left house, farm, wife and child and went with him to the war."

She had told it timidly with failing voice like a truthful man lying. After that she looked tensely at her mother.

Her mother thought about it for a while.

"I don't think so," she replied distractedly.

"Now, think about it," Leonore urged firmly.

"Why then, what is there in this story for you today?"

"Yes, it's doesn't matter how it went," Griebel endorsed her.

"But, it would please me so, mother. I just want to see if I have remembered it!"

"Oh leave it," her mother parried, as she scented some unpleasant consequence.

Leonore insisted more and more ardently on her request, and in the end tears entered her eyes.

"Now wait, if there's so much in it ... right! —
yes, yes, now I have it!"

"Do you, mother!" the poor woman called
overjoyed.

"Now listen, Joseph, you will see!"

"Yes, the first half of it was there in what you
told. But then it is different." With that the old
woman took a serious pose and with singing
melody, she told the following: — "Then the big,
rich emperor came to the poor knight and said,
'The steeds of my enemy are drinking from the
streams of your fatherland, my empire. Stand up
and go forth from the house of your father and
your wife who you so love.

Sacrifice yourself and your two year old son
for the holy cause of his emperor.'

'And why my son too?' asked the knight
astounded.

'Because I cherish you like my armour, I don't
want you cast away from me because of your
bold question. A wise woman met me once in the
forest where I had lost my way during the hunt,
and she showed me the right path. When she
learnt who I was, she looked in my hand and
said, grim days will one day feed in your heart
with the bloody teeth of war.

The strength of your army will not be enough
then against that of your enemy. Then desire the
suckling boy of a knight whose soul is faithful to
you like the breath of spring to your mouth. Kill

his child and have all the knights dip their swords in his innocent blood.

Then a fervent hunger will come over the weapons so that they mow your enemies down like the grass falling under the farmer's scythe.

Because you are dearer to me than anyone else, I desire your little son. It is a matter of heaven. If you assent then you are first after me in my empire.'

Then the knight said, while he looked at his wife shaking in anguish ..."

The story was broken off.

"Marsel-mother, you should be going home soon, may I say. It's time for turning in," the rumbling voice of Anna called through the door.

"Jesus yes, we've been talking too much, it's already past eight, almost nine. Good night! Stay at peace with each other, and Lorie, don't always fall ill straightaway."

She kissed her daughter on the forehead and threatened her seriously with her finger.

Motionless, her elbows propped on the table, she sat there. The caresses of her mother only evoked a distracted smile on her face, and she did not notice that her husband accompanied the parting woman into the hall, where they whispered to each other — — — — — — — —

Suddenly she sprang up and snatched at the air while she threw her arm up ...

Her husband's step, which became louder and louder in the hall, pressed her onto her chair again, and a repugnance distorted her face like it besets the famished before a meal. With lack-lustre faces, they look at it: it is already too late ... oh, if everything had come moments earlier, when their hunger still had the power of yearning; but now! —

Her husband entered, a bottle of wine in his arm, two glasses in his hand, a tantalising grin over his entire face.

"Aren't you hungry, Lorla?"

Without looking at him, she shook her head heavily.

"Me neither. — Come, today we'll make a thick belly empty. — Isn't it like a festive day?"

She remained in silent seclusion.

He poured, and the perfumed pearls of wine settled down singing in the glasses.

"Cheers!"

Griebel knocked against the glass which he had placed in front of his wife.

"Drink! — Listen how it sounds, bright like when you laugh."

It had to come to conciliation; it was definite with him. "I'll make the table clean entirely alone," he had said in the hall, not without a touch of boasting.

"Now, it's not poison!" he took it up again. "Look at me. In one gulp. — Woop, away it goes!

— Perhaps you'll drink a toast with a second. —
Cheers, Lorla! Don't be a frog! Wine gladdens the
heart. Isn't it so? —"

Again he hastily emptied his glass and poured
another. For now it should 'proceed from here'.
"Isn't it so?" he repeated, after seeking a talking
point. He did not find any and lumbered on
blindly,

"Jesus no, am I a ...? — What is it then? Does
the world need to know what we have? —

Am I not a good fellow, hey?

Lord God! Is a word a roll of cloth? —

I assume: I'll bring something up in the city
council. I don't want to — I'll complain — I'm a
city councillor — I can — I'll publicise it ... Good
for the thing! ... It's the water pipe, the footpath
on the inner side of the Ring, the paving,
something. — Good! — I have my reasons, you
understand, for I wasn't born yesterday! No! In
detail, I'll say everything so it can be grasped
exactly. If it doesn't go through: won't do any
more damage. Will I bed in the cellar because of
it? No!

Now, Lorla, isn't everything in the world as
people want it?"

He said it with great determination and per-
suasiveness, in stanzas which worked themselves
weightily out of long pauses.

But on Leonore, it all made not the least impression. She had propped her head on her left hand and was staring up at the ceiling.

Griebel poured himself a third and drank it.

"What's on the ceiling then, Lorla? — Oh, a nest of cobwebs! — No, you dear women only ever have scraping and cleaning on your minds when you're on your feet."

He had to get her talking. The rest would soon be found out. He would then process everything that came to light with his "bright mind".

"Hmmm!"

Finally Leonore let out a meditative sound.

Then she turned with stiff upper body quietly to him,

"Don't you want to hear more of the story mother was telling?"

"Of course, the story, certainly. Look, I really do!"

These words brought a cutting, self-critical smile to her face. Resignedly she turned away as she answered,

"... You? ... you! ..."

But she did not say it fervently threatening as before. Wilted, cold, as if she was exuding heavy drops which, now ashes, once blisteringly seared her tongue.

After a long look into emptiness, it started against her will, like you would tell the dream of a lost life — — — — — "... the knight drank his wife with his eyes ... Then he knelt down before the emperor, 'Take my sword, my honour — your favour — my little son, everything, — everything!! — only ... leave me ... my ... wife —"

A long, mysterious sound, as though her soul was groaning without availing bodily organs, concluded these words.

Now the moment of decision was here, the moment to which she had been struggling with the trembling confusion of her restless marriage.

Half in falling, half in jumping up, she hung to the edge of her chair.

Griebel thought the story would not last much longer and waited comfortably for the end. Since it was not forthcoming, he wanted to tell a story himself to fortify the advantage he had obtained,

"Now listen, I'll tell you something here: My father was walking, it was ..."

"Now that's it! Now I must go ... perhaps to him ... who knows ... now I must ... now ... now ..."

A fatal stroke had robbed her of thought. With horror, she had sprung up. Now, grasping about confusedly, she rushed through the room.

Griebel did not understand how she came up with this "foolishness",

"Just don't scream again. Try to pull yourself together and sit down, I'll tell you a story ..."

At these words, a rigidity came over her. At the portière to the bedroom door, she turned around and looked at Griebel from the side with raw astonishment. — He sat there in embarrassment, swirling in held breath his good teachings and sipping his wine. — After a short struggle with herself, Leonore slowly approached the table.

As she now seemed so grave, Griebel drew back before her deathly pale face with its large, despairing eyes.

"Griebel, Joseph, I'm going, as otherwise I'll die," she said exhausted.

In his helplessness, he clung solely to her words as though to make himself numb against all the fears which were bothering him like a swarm of midges.

"You die; so healthy and strong."

"Even despite that. Healthy people die; sick people just close their eyes."

"I'm going!" she asserted after a while, calming her trembling excitement, since Griebel sat there saying nothing.

"And the child, little Gustav, our boy?" he recovered.

"He isn't mine."

"Now in all the world, who does he belong to?"

"He's yours, simply yours, all alone."

She poured a smile, in which she besmirched herself lustfully, with cold lips quietly into her heart.

"Truly my poor soul!" she ardently placed her right hand on her heart. "For you aren't good to me. I did not, never had you, never! That's why ... and that's why I am really a human being, because I nevertheless became little Gustav's mother ... a whore ... that's also why I can go. For nothing by a human being is bad."

"Aren't I good to you, Lorla, aren't I?!"

Hastily he stretched out his fleshy hand, and his kind face trembled in fright.

"Why, or how do you want to prove it?"

"Aren't you my wife? Didn't I marry you, hey? — I work for you. Have you once gone hungry, not had everything you wanted: dresses, rooms, the house full of things, money, how much do you want? — Well? Do I torture you? Do I scream? — do I drink? — am I a hound?"

He swallowed each of these cries like a fortifying morsel.

Then he sprang up, hastily emptied his glass, shoved it down hard and was now looking at her reflectively. "... it's all true. Rather *too* much, too much ..."

After these words, Leonore stared at the table. Her thoughts began emptying themselves again in painfully surging impotence, she was starting to sink down.

"No!"

With hard self-derision, she whipped herself up.

"Why should I stay then? Now that I have it all!"

Again she broke off stiffly into a fervidly begun gesture of flight, "My mother!! — But what is the use? — I'm perishing, and who's helping me? Not me, not you, nobody! — And was it necessary that I should be so unhappy, in fear, in peace, in happiness, in ... Jesus Maria, forgive me my sins!"

All the terrible things which brought her to despair in lonely torture were bearing down on her at once.

With staggering knees, she came to the point of her rescue, with blazing breath, turbid heartbeat and torn up thoughts.

"Apart! — Away! — Here, the wedding ring ... the jacket is also from you ... the skirt too ... the bodice and everything ... everything ... everything ... here, Joseph Griebel, take it, I can, I am ..."

Shivering she stripped off all the things he had bought her. With her dresses, she was discarding all the sweet delusions, all the beliefs in the imperatives of men. The trembling waves of her delicate bosom swelled through the cleavage of her top like shimmering waves shake when they meet the first cold light of a new day.

"Now your love is lying there on the table — a paltry bundle ... Only that is mine."

She unfastened her hair so that it glided down over her shoulders like golden sunlight. With soft fingers, she caressed it. But now she did not know anymore what she wanted; with a lost smile, she stood there.

Griebel's consternation over this shocking change flowed into fervent pity when he saw this tender, beautiful being shaking with her misery. The wine also widened the pupils of his emotion.

An abruptly flaring, wild stream ravished him. He enveloped her with a strong, decisive grip — covering her half exposed body with kisses, he stammered with the untoward lips of desire, "Lorie, dear, dearest Lorie! — Don't be silly, I'm good to you, how I'm good to you! — Stay with me!"

In the gliding away into another world, he tore her back again. She struggled wildly against him, already under the spell of new morals; but he recklessly embraced her arms with a powerful envelopment of her body.

Thus, the morbid rambling thrown back into her hungering heart, a blazing fire was sparked in it. The unruliness of his passion gave her the sacrificial radiance of succumbing.

Slowly her hardness turned into cuddles, her profanities into quiet jubilation,

"My sweetheart!"

With gentle care, he took her into his bed ... — — — The silent desire of her full maturity was fulfilled, the discord of her spiritual desire was submerged in the testifying steady rhythm of her blood. — For all the mental powers of the woman are physical, and her body is the complete fullness of her soul ... the tingling of her excited blood was flowing like childlike sweetness into her consciousness.

They then lay for a long time in motionless embrace under the unmistaken power of a storm carrying them away.

They drank long kisses, soft and cautious, as if they were plucking precious flowers from swaying stems. With wide, gleaming eyes, Leonore enjoyed that veiled intoxication of images which such quieter waves of joy bring playing within themselves.

The table lamp was still burning in the sitting room next to them. The red portière obstructed the light's entry so much that only a fine web of weary radiant threads hung powerless in the darkness of the bedroom. Only a pointed zigzagging strip of light stretched obliquely to the wall over the head of the bed which stood to the right by the door. In comparison to the softly blurring twilight of the rest of the room, this clear light was merciless, cold.

Leonore could not observe it without unease. She had checked it a few times already, but always turned around again hastily, and asked passionately, "Completely, completely?"

"Yes, completely," Griebel answered patiently until his voice started to assume an impatient aspect. Only she was not accepting that; for when she, half turned away, perceived the shimmering play of the hard waves of light again, she felt compelled to ask her husband anew for confirmation of his love, as if a doubt was flickering across from there.

"But now I see it exactly," she said decisively and turned to the strip of light.

"What then?" Griebel asked after a while distractedly.

"Now, the light. — It is odd actually, when you think about it," she began after a while dreamily.

"What?"

"The light there."

"Oh! — The lamp's still burning on the table. The light's just coming into the room from in-between the curtains. It's no odder than that!"

"... oh yes —" she lay there with half-closed eyes and a shiver quietly ran through her limbs, like it does with children listening to a fairy tale ... "truly, as if it was a different realm out there and here too ... My mother told me a story about the mermaid — — the biting, hard sun of the day — when the eyes hurt, the tongue becomes seared for thirst, where people become tired and old in the dust, where it is either freezing cold or perishingly hot ...

The little boy was then caught by a pain as though his soul was homesick.

And he walked to the still water in the green darkness. The white water lilies were swimming silently in the pond, their gleaming leaves lay sleeping inaudibly around them. In the air above them, a motionless spell hung.

The boy looked at it for a long time with his eyes weary from the light, and his heart unlocked the spell since it was pure.

The water lilies turned into sweet, white, smiling faces, the leaves changed into green garments, and the pale reddish stems rose like slender limbs from the soft, still water. The spell came alive in the air and a singing wind drew mysterious circles across the flat surface on which the mermaids danced so that their golden green hair fluttered.

And the boy sank under the water out of the light ... are you asleep already, Joseph?"

"No —"

"You were, I am not that dumb. But the little story occurred to me straightaway. Well, why couldn't it be so? See, I'm the mermaid and you are the boy. The strip of light there across the wall to the floor is the bridge to the earth ..."

With that she sprang out of bed, ran into the sitting room and blew out the lamp.

Then she knelt next to him,

"Now you can't get away from me anymore, as the bridge has collapsed. Now you are mine forever. Sleep, sleep, you are tired of the light. I will cover you up with my hair."

Softly she let the rich flood of her hair fall over his body, bent down and kissed his face with her delicate mouth.

"Oh — get your hair away! It tickles like a thousand fleas."

"Yes, yes. You're right, I won't let you sleep. Be good, it was merely fun. I am still the pure child, aren't I. — Good night! — Love you! — Kiss me! — lots, lots!"

"Now's good though, Lorla, isn't it? — See, but now we must sleep."

— — — —

"Dear! — Are you really good to me?"

"Oh now indeed. But now we should let the questions be."

She obediently let it pass.

But her unrest drove her to her husband anew,

"Put your arms around me!"

In answer Griebel moved hastily without a word — from her longing arms towards the wall and settled himself intricately into some peace with unhurried snoring noises like a plump animal. At the same time a sharp, pickling smell came from his body.

All that penetrated Leonore like a cut so that an unspeakable languor came over her. At the same time, she had the certainty of having to scream if she stirred. She lay quite, quite motionless. Her breathing was quick and hot. That terrible sound with which it came was torturing her. A few times, she swallowed it down; but ardently, with trembling breast, she then strove against it again. Fuss and anxiety was coming over her. Her heart was pounding. In terror she sprang up onto her knees.

Now she seemed to have escaped the spell of this thought. Full of courage, she shook her head and looked at her husband lying next to her. She knew that she could not see him. She just wanted to hear more keenly.

"No, he cannot deceive me, no — no ..."

She said it shivering like when on an wintry night you wrap a thin garment around your shoulders and, gazing into the forest, lie to yourself, "No, it isn't cold."

Griebel's fat snoring sounds began, a sign that he was fast asleep. She had to imagine a big, gleaming face, as the lips of his half-open mouth were sucked in dragging and pushed out sputtering, with his blond moustache bristling erect each time.

"He is sleeping like after work." This thought assaulted her in fright.

Where has the sweetness gone, his cuddles, his soft love. The house is speaking stricken, long tones. Sometimes they break off brusquely, and then her thoughts are startled by a weight that comes over them, agitated.

"The wind will be coming ..." she stuttered to herself and listened in flight from herself.

Then it was completely still, and she calmed her breathing down while she pressed her fist against her heart so that it was half buried in her bosom. For the waves of this air in her trembling breast were pressing down on her like an inconsiderate confirmation of her need for help, as if she was swaying, groaning like an uprooted sapling.

Then a wavering strip glided through the dark room, as if the wings of a drowsy fly were beating towards an object. Perhaps it was the snowflakes sinking down on the windowpanes.

"A mysterious night, this night."

She said "this night" to demonstrate to herself how important it was to listen to everything.

In reality she was only fleeing from the certainty that was arising painfully in her.

The night watchman was whistling the tenth hour. The tones spaced themselves out wearily one after the other. After that rhythmically departing steps could be heard.

"Like a big clock sounding the same steps."

She thought about it with the same fleeting attentiveness.

Suddenly it occurred to her that she could not hear the clock in the hall. —

No ...

Her mother had often told of how the wall clock had stopped before the death of her father.

Truly, the clock out there was not going anymore. What sort of misfortune did that mean?

The fumes of the wine, which attracted her attention at the same moment, removed every doubt.

"It was only the intoxication, and none of it is true ..."

He had deceived her, and how she had given herself to him! Now he was lying there, and in the morning he would laugh at her, and her holiest despair melted away again into the gutter of the everyday like so much else.

In futile consternation, she fell across him and jogged his shoulder.

"Joseph! — Joseph!"

She could not live so. — "Joseph!"

"What's it now then?"

He raised himself half up dully and yawned.

"Go and wash your eyes with cold water!"

She exclaimed it in great excitement.

Her voice's sound was so convulsive that the cloth maker became fully awake and asked full of worry, "Hey, dear Lorla, ha, what's it then now!? Have you had a bad dream?"

Trembling she grasped for his hands, let them go, however, and huddled against his chest.

"Take me in your arms, tight — tighter! — Kiss me!" Under his loving caresses, her breath was becoming more regular, her heart calmer. She shut her eyes and gave herself up exhausted to a sweet, soft security.

But Griebel was falling asleep again already. Since Leonore was not stirring, he cautiously let his arm sink to quietly cushion her motionless body which he believed was already under the spell of sleep.

Then she started sharply and asked in fervent haste, "Dear, do you lie too? — Have you ever deceived me in your life?"

"What that now again," Griebel thought and said loudly, "No! — But isn't there time for this tomorrow?"

"Dear, on your conscience, I'm asking you!"

"No," he repeated, becoming uncertain as a result of the serious ring in the tone of her voice.

"Do you want to tell me the truth now? — From the bottom of your heart, pure and all"

"Yes, the lot, say what you want!"

"Are you good to me?"

"Yes."

"Completely?"

"Yes."

"Hallowed, like the moonlight is?"

"Yes."

"Like silvery, sweet, pure water?"

"Yes."

"Like bells ringing ... like the blue world of heaven over the mountains ... like the deep red in the evening clouds ... for years ... an eternity? ..."

She had stopped listening for an answer. The fervour of the yearning for life which was embracing the ardency of her love of life was spreading an ecstasy over her soul. Her words, which, like the lines of a song, flowed ecstatically from her lips, dying away slowly like wafting notes, brought an infinitely deep intoxicating certainty over her. In unmoving bliss, she then listened to the fading away of her voice and did not notice that Griebel had already lain down again. He held his breath, thinking amusedly, "Well, now I just want to see how long she will prattle on for!" and stayed still while Leonore still knelt next to him as though turned to stone.

—

Finally he could not hold his breath any longer, and with crashing laughter, he let it out, "Haha! — Thunderbolts! — What ideas you have! — Now in the middle of the night, you begin and act like a little singing maid — lo*oong* and hi*iigh*!" He mimicked her thus.

Vacantly, clumsily, he laughed at her. — — —

Only, during his laughter, he heard a fine, infinitely raw tone turning into a loud wailing and stopping shrilly as though a golden string had been torn in two.

At the same time, he felt Leonore's calf, which lay on his chest, trembling more and more.

It turned into a shivering.

Startled he sat up.

His wife had collapsed and had buried her head in the pillow. She was murmuring something and grasping the bed in convulsions ever anew like someone foundering.

"I was just having a little fun," Griebel thought and dully felt a great guilt. That's why he did not speak.

Now Leonore was straightening up, and he felt her hand falling heavily onto his chest. It was balled into a fist, cold and hard like a stone. She was quite subtly twitching. She lay there stiffly for a long time. Then she began pressing more and more. When her joint crunched over, she slackened the pressure for a while. Suddenly she placed the other hand next to it, also balled into a fist, cold and hard as stone.

Now she was driving her fists into the fat of his chest as though her knuckles were merciless teeth.

Already Griebel was feeling a burning pain in that place. A blind fear commanded him not to stir in order not to excite her temper.

Finally he could not endure it anymore.

Quietly he began to glide out from under the pressure of the rigid fists.

But as soon as the first movement of his body occurred, her fury broke forth.

She bore down on him, choked him, struck his face with her fists and tore at his hair. At the same time, she screamed misshapenly,

"Dog! ... dog!! — ha! ... tear my body apart! — You must, you must! I have swallowed my shame — — you have made me human for the second time!"

This cry climbed from the rattling of incurable wounds.

Yet Griebel was only defending himself weakly, although he already felt it running hot over his face, because he thought that he deserved it.

Suddenly Leonore was attacked by the fear of a wild beast meeting its death, and she felt irrecoverably lost. Gritting, she thrust herself on him again and dug her fingers clutching around his throat,

"So you die too!" —

Griebel was suffocating. The last multi-coloured wheel before his eyes danced into the night, and music rose in his ears. The lust for death arose in his lower body ...

Then he cast her aside with a terrible shove so that she flew from the bed and slammed down dully.

A chair fell crashing over.

Then there was a grave silence.

The shadows of the night did not stir.

After a while, the door to the sitting room creaked.

A cautious shuffling went into the hall.

CHAPTER 14

Leonore Griebel

Now the bells had died away, forever. A trembling tone resided in the entire house the next morning.

Leonore had been working assiduously in the kitchen since the early morning hours. She was morbidly hungry for work. Especially noisy activities did her good: the getting in of the coal, the whining awakening of the crockery, the crunching of the revolving coffee grinder. She grasped every object hastily and shook them as though throwing them from her hand. Suddenly, standing in the middle of the kitchen, she started,

"Be quiet, girls! — No, listen!"

"Jesus, Mrs Griebel, you have a completely different voice! How do you talk like that?"

"How what?"

"Well, as it seems to me ..."

"Oh, Anna, that's all, all the same. — But don't you hear it? — The wind ... the wind ... a wind ..."

"Oh now, it is turning into spring, Mrs Griebel, it is. Spring wind. Don't you hear how it goes?" the nurse explained embarrassed.

Terrified, Leonore looked at her, but immediately lowered her gaze in confusion, shook her head in denial, murmured something and quickly left the kitchen. She crept on her toes to the nursery and leant her ear to the wall of the bedroom. She only heard very indistinctly the step of her husband. She remained huddled up for a long time. The uncomfortable position gave her pains in the back and legs which continually increased. But she did not stand up.

If she were to break her backbone so that she could die in agony ...

She smiled happily over that and doubled over still more, just like a bundle of worn clothes lying on the floor.

Only she had to rise again.

Slowly, despondently she went back to the kitchen, over to the clock which had not yet been set going again.

Leonore started when she noticed that the hand was showing fifteen minutes after seven.

But she did not deny to herself knowing why she was horrified.

Carefully, so that nobody heard, she wound the clock and set it. When the pendulum was again emitting its eternally regular ticking in leisurely swings, the tears entered her eyes and she crept away bowed down.

In the kitchen, an empty attentiveness came over her. With unknowing eyes, she looked at everything going on, tore the tray with the crockery for breakfast from Anna's hands and carried it with stiffly dragging steps to the sitting room. The girl opened the door for her. Leonore looked just then into the open room in which a timid morning light resided and from which the fumes of wine were blowing towards her. It seemed to her as if she would have to throw everything down and run away. A silent force, however, shoved her in with a clumsy hand.

Griebel, who stood half dressed before the mirror and was observing his neck, turned around hastily and hurried with powerful strides into the bedroom.

The bloody marks and stripes on his neck and the many-coloured bulging bruises on his face had not escaped Leonore's timidly trembling gaze. It turned black before her eyes and her entire body shook.

Then a dumb, numbed peace came over her. Standing stiffly at the table, her lips pressed together, she stood with wide eyes for a long time motionless and observed with beastly stupid attentiveness the crockery lying before her, the bulbous wine bottle, the ring with the red stone. "Now I must go again," it feebly came over her. Her arms fell slackly down by her body. With weary steps, she went out.

A wilted, disconsolate wistfulness lay on her all day. In gripping things she sometimes came to a dull self-assurance which did not hurt her.

Then she sat motionless and her eyes were as though broken.

The next day, which was before the feast of the annunciation which fell on a Sunday, she went to confession. She did it without ever losing the numbness in which her anxiety was stirring the way a single rotten leaf waves up and down whirring in dead, immense dreariness.

She sought out the confessional which stood deep in the darkest corner under the chancel, and she fell to her knees before the grate.

The white hand of the clergyman made the cross. Then he dipped his ear down.

A trembling agitation came over Leonore as she pressed her pale face hard against the bars of the grate, and she thought, "If I could die now."

This thought returned the initial emptiness and stiffness to her so that she forgot everything and emitted only short, gasping breaths.

The clergyman finally bent down and looked her in the face. Two forlorn, rigid eyes, of which one drooped soulless to the side, shocked him.

"Go home, you are sick," he whispered.

"Not absolved? no?" she stuttered in deepest mortal fear.

"Then confess!"

"... I ... wanted, wanted ... to strangle my husband ... but my soul was only a wound ... Father, have mercy ... my poor soul ..." she murmured turbidly with gritted teeth.

The clergyman saw her despair, bent down and dismissed her with a gracious sign, for he had known her a long time.

Then the poor thing staggered out.

Without break, agonising, heavy fears were coming over her from the colourless, cold wreckage of her irrecoverably lost soul, which, formerly a magically incorporeal world, had changed into a terrible hurricane in a dreary waste.

Her consciousness swayed in it like a wispy, seedless stalk, and rescued itself in the dead rhythm of hard work.

But in her deserted depths, a restless trembling was cowering unable to be dislodged, an eyeless fear which beset her even worse during clear, loud speech.

That's why she fell silent more and more until she only talked with weak, trembling motions of her head, a tired countenance, with the slack play of her overlong arms.

In the end, Leonore also found a place where she could rest from her misery.

In the midst of the befuddlement of action, a dreary boundlessness arose in her, and a surging addiction was seizing her, a roving spirit that hammered her pulse covetously. When she attempted to stand up to this blind aggression, her breath failed her, a torturous unease confused the uninspired harmony of her activity.

That's why she let everything lie and began a confused, pointless rambling through the broad house. The multifaceted circumstances, reflexes, moods and sounds through which she hurried produced in her the delusion of an emotional argument for which she had neither the power of courage nor the strength.

In the end then, the house's complex rested in her like a private world. The beat of her heart was wandering under the spell of fixed poles.

The expellee from the destruction of her inner being emigrated in blind convulsions and found with the pitiful remnants of her desolated world a home for her soul in the soulless house. It took her in its broad, stony arms and cradled her in mysterious silence.

Once, in the days of her agonising sun's rising, it had dismissed the play of a young heart with its dignified, grumpy grey like an old man's brow scares away the play of children. Now it lured the woman to itself with quiet, peaceful sounds so that she was silenced by it and learnt a dreamless slumber after the shipwreck of her life.

The house became her body, and when she went away from its wrapper, she felt the torments of an invalid tearing the bandages from his incurable wounds. Hounded, she hurried through the streets. Every curious look was a merciless stab to her, every laugh corrosive poison, every greeting an accusation, and every conversation torture for a confession.

When, breathing out, she reentered the house, she shuffled with tired, dragging steps the feeling of a peaceful self-acceptance into herself. Her sashaying garment then released a whispering breeze around her as if a good, strong friend was walking invisibly next to her and purring calming murmurings into her heart.

But the house is also becoming her soul.

Everything which had eternally foundered in her, everything which had been lost forever, wells out of the house into her. It is high, stiff and cold like her inner being. Many broad, unliveable, deserted rooms are in her, packed full like the rooms of the house with now useless things, and the mouldy smell of a lost time lay around everything.

Shapeless shadows are strolling through her. Icy fear crawls up the bleakness of high walls and falls gliding to the floor.

Once something acted in them, something mirthful, in searching desire, with pounding heart, enraptured dreams, unchained ferocity. Who still knows it today?

All that life now lies as dust on the rotten things of this wrecked time. Nobody stirs it up, from awe of the ghosts of the past, from an awe which is perhaps the last desire encountered at death.

Thus Leonore rests in the satiety of this great peace. It seems to her as though something distant, never seen, is moving in her once more when long, vague sounds waft up the broad stairs.

The thunder, which the rising storm blasts from its thick walls, seizes her like a shocking incident. The dust dancing in the sunlight of the garret is her dream. The story of her youth resides in the boxes and chests. With the creaking swing of the door she is startled and submits to the regular sound of deep solitude which fills every corner of the house mumbling monotonously and glides in and out through every crook and cranny.

Only the lion's head at the end of the stairs roars with throat wide open in silent, distorted fury, although the crust of age crouches in the corners of its eyes as though fear and trembling cowers in their depths and never leaves them.

This hidden life was pulsing within her. But nobody could understand it.

It suckled on her. Her fullness declined. The waves of her bosom dried out. The skin of her lean face became white as paper. Her hair obtained a brittle, grey-blond colour. The gentle way of her pale blue eyes had long been silenced.

Wilted and rotten in the midst of the waves of laughing human time, it was as though she came into the world without any youth.

For a long time, she had again been living an everyday life with her husband.

After they had timidly avoided each other, "it had happened by itself." She did not know "how they had come together again."

But they talked to each other over a line which no one crossed.

They consorted with each other like friends who are hiding a jointly committed crime.

At times Leonore had relapses. Once when she came out of the cellar with a pot full of potatoes in her hand, the front door had been opened by someone and not closed again. Golden sunlight was streaming in jubilantly and immersing her in shimmering happiness.

Then Leonore let the pot fall in dismay and, whilst her heart began beating painfully as if it wanted to tear itself from its chains, she fled into the twilight of the hall.

When birdsong sounded from the garden into the kitchen, she paled and shut the window hurriedly.

After a lunch, she was sitting quietly and leisurely chewing the last morsel when Griebel floundered into a story from her past. He was looking down in front of him as he spoke.

A deep groaning startled him from his casual talkativeness.

His wife was sitting there as though she was breathing a paralysing poison, stiffly, and her eyes were staring motionless at the air as though she was seeing a ghost.

He immediately broke off stuttering.

They sat opposite each other for a long time and clung on to each other with silent looks. Like children look at each other when a fearful noise brings them to consciousness in the middle of the terrible night. Their skin pimples in the frost of fear, and an icy breath wafts into their deepest soul. When the horror fatigues them, they cautiously fall down and creep away into the shelter of sleep.

Leonore and Griebel crept away from each other after a while and ensconced themselves in the closeness of their empty existence.

On the night of a full moon, Leonore started from the beginnings of sleep and vigorously shook her husband awake.

"If it were just a boy again, that I could bear," she said to him softly.

"Oh no, we have a boy already, woman. Now I'd really prefer a girl," Griebel replied.

"Oh, blessed heaven! Griebel, a girl! Do you know what a girl is? Oh, Maria, don't sin against your child and me. I pray day and night for it."

Her voice died away.

Then, for a long time, only the couple's sorrowful breathing could be heard.

"He must become a clergyman," Leonore finally began still timider.

"It isn't simple 'to become' one. You need to have a clever head for that. Yes. But who knows?"

"He must! — He must!" Leonore exclaimed in great distress.

"Well, he 'must', how silly you talk! We don't have that in our power!"

"He must!" the poor woman repeated in obstinate hardheadedness. "Because Griebel, what use has your prayer had since it happened with us? Look, but if a pure child prays to Our Father in heaven for us two poor people, then he can perhaps help us again out of our hardship." —

W eak trees cast off their fruit prematurely. The child's birth occurred a month too early. But Leonore's fate had listened to her secret sobbing for the first time: it was a boy again, and he received the names Josephus Arnestus and was strong and healthy despite his early arrival, as he had absorbed all the dormant strength of the maternal body.

She was left behind like an empty basin.

After many months, Leonore was invigorated enough that she could be packed into a carriage and sent to a small neighbouring spa whose waters "worked wonders with women's complaints".

Griebel, who led her down the stairs, did not sense Leonore's opposition. He only felt her hand trembling and saw solitary tears slowly trickling from her almost extinguished eyes.

When they were already quite close to the spa and could see the red tower of its newly built church over the tips of the trees, Griebel pointed with outstretched arm in that direction and said,

"Do you see, there's Kudowa already!"

Leonore abruptly lifted up her emaciated little head on its thin neck as though in fright. Then she fell back despondently. As she was rocked back and forth by the motion of the carriage, her lips murmured the same words continually, lacklustre and dying away,

"There — I'll — cer—tainly — die ..."

"No, you'll get well there, Lorla. That's what spas are for, not for dying," Griebel answered, having finally understood her.

Leonore shook her head with the last forces of her defence and then lapsed into dreamlike impotence.

She was carried thus into her quiet room, whose windows looked out on the loneliest part of the small park. —

Obediently, like a well-behaved child, with the perpetually unchanging, wilted, sniveling smile in her blue-white face, she carried out all the orders of the worried doctor, who was astonished at the resilience of her emaciated body.

There was just one thing he could not understand. Whenever he warmly and happily promised her an early walk, she became quite distressed and looked at him, begging through tears for mercy.

Once she was particularly vigorous, saying,

"I will not bear it, doctor. I know I cannot bear it."

"Oh no, dear Mrs Griebel, the sun works wonders, and the people you'll see will distract you too. Such things are invigorating."

"No, no! Even the sun, people, life, I can't bear life anymore ... even that ... it is ... even that."

Her words dwindled away into a rigidity as though she was thinking about things, about chairs, paving stones, uninhabited houses.

The doctor talked to her more insistently in order to convince her. But she did not seem to understand anything anymore.

Immovable, she looked down before her.

On a mild, quiet, early morning, her attendant led her into the park.

The band was just then playing the beginning of its second piece when she entered the broad avenue which ended at a small pond shimmering in the green-dawning expanse and dreaming fine mist in the young light.

Timidly, with eyes directed at the ground, Leonore crept there. Her breaths were deep and irregular. Her arm weighed heavier and heavier on that of her attendant, and she often stumbled over her own feet.

Leonore Griebel

Some hundred steps in front of her, a young married couple were strolling. The woman in her bright dress and red silk blouse nestled closely to her husband, and her little head rocked in time to the music.

The attendant, plump like a turnip, called her attention to the couple,

"Look, Mrs Griebel, they're certainly better."

Exhausted, Leonore stopped and looked up.

"There, I mean them," the attendant repeated.

At that moment, the couple swivelled around and the young woman flew with happy laughter into the open arms of her husband who squeezed her to himself whilst giving her a long kiss.

With a bone-chilling scream, Leonore broke down and collapsed. — —

The usual affair immediately unfolded.

From every corner, curious people came running and stood around this unfortunate woman lying lifeless on the ground. Everyone was helping with loud advice, nobody was lending a hand. The women wailed and lamented. — The plump turnip shook Leonore repeatedly and constantly moaned tearfully,

"I can't lift her alone. — Dear sir, would you be so good and carry her! — Just look, dear lady, she is dying. What will the doctor say when a guest dies on the grounds in broad daylight!"

Finally a servant appeared with a wheelchair. The patient was placed in it and taken to her apartment.

In excited chatter, the audience dispersed and berated the irresponsible recklessness of the doctor in allowing "this dangerously ill person" out.

Leonore was recklessly sent home the next day so that she would not die in the spa.

But the deep sounds of the austere house on the Walkergasse, the bleak, high spaces, the heavy shadows all worked wonders.

She again became so strong that she could sit upright in an armchair and move slowly with a walking stick.

But most of the time, she sat in the armchair, let the beads of the rosary glide through her withered hands and ceaselessly moved her thin, pale lips.

She was praying for her sins.

She never spoke a word against anyone anymore.

With the entrance of her husband, she did not stir.

Only the small talk of her old mother sometimes brought a light into her sunken eyes, which looked like the glimmer of a decayed house's broken windowpanes in the tired moonlight. —

Leonore Griebel

After many, many years, in an autumn night, she expired silently and alone next to her sleeping husband.

About the Publisher

Our mission is to provide translations into English of the complete works of neglected major European writers. We do not cherry-pick works that seem the most marketable, but rather seek to provide a complete collection of each writer's works so that readers can follow the writer's development and decide on its merits for themselves.